Heartbeat Drumbeat

Irene Beltrán Hernández

Arte Público Press
Houston
Texas
1992

This book is made possible through a grant from the National Endowment for the Arts, a federal agency.

Arte Público Press
University of Houston
Houston, Texas 77204-2090

Cover design by Mark Piñón

Hernández, Irene Beltrán, 1945–
    Heartbeat Drumbeat / by Irene Beltrán Hernández.
        p.   cm.
    Summary: A young woman finds the course of her life influenced by her Navajo and Mexican heritages and especially by an older Navajo woman and a young Indian lawyer.
    ISBN 1-55885-052-X
    1. Navajo Indians—Juvenile fiction. [1. Navajo Indians—Fiction. 2. Indians of North America—Fiction.] I. Title.
PZ7.H43175He 1992
[Fic]—dc20   91-48246
                                                                                CIP
                                                                                AC

The paper used in this publication meets the requirements of the American National Standard for Permanence of Paper for Printed Library Materials Z39.48-1984. ∞

Heartbeat Drumbeat is dedicated to two people:

Olga Evanoff, who worked with me through many revisions. I appreciate her confidence, her influence and her tireless patience.

And my husband, Gilberto Rolando Hernández, who is more Indian than Mexican.

Irene Beltrán Hernández

Heartbeat Drumbeat

Chapter 1

The coldness crept upon Morgana, as did the man in her dream. The man with the golden eyes, the expensive boots, and the fragrance of new leather. He called her urgently. He is Indian, she thought, noticing that his black hair was braided into long plaits. He was not smiling; yet, one corner of his mouth was pulled up in a mischievous manner. With his left hand he beckoned her, while his other hand quickly placed a black Stetson upon his head. In the palm of his outstretched hand, he held an object which shone like the silver moon, its rays spellbinding. She held her arm outstretched to take the thick bracelet of gleaming silver, but he withdrew his palm. Slowly, he opened his palm and pitched the bracelet as far as he could into the dark crevices of the deep canyon below.

She screamed, "That was my mother's bracelet!"

He quickly declared, "She is dead. She no longer needs her possessions ... so says Navajo law."

Numbness overtook Morgana as images of her mother, Marisol, flashed before her mind like a shuffled deck of cards. "My mother lives!" she retaliated, wishing more than anything she could shove him over the edge of the cliff. "Tell me who you are and how you got my mother's bracelet."

He laughed and stepped closer toward her.

Morgana Cruz woke from her dream instantly. She pulled the blanket tightly around her, trying to shake the dream from her mind. Why be afraid, she reasoned. Wasn't she in her own room, a room she'd known since her birth? A room that held no granite cliffs. Still, she was frightened. The bracelet in her dream she recognized as an antique that her father had given to her mother as a wedding present. Marisol, she knew for a fact, was alive and sleeping soundly in the room below hers.

Isadora, her Navajo mentor, had taught her that dreams were peepholes into the future. Do not fear dreams, Isadora had said, but remember them and seek clues to enlighten the coming events. Yes, that is what she should do—seek clues, but still she was frightened of the man, of the dream, and of the warning that her mother was to die.

Morgana pressed a lace pillow tightly over her heart, not daring to move until the first rays of daylight appeared through her balcony doors. Only then did she allow herself to drift into an exhausted sleep.

♡   ♡   ♡

Morgana awoke late. Feeling trapped by her dream as if she'd been hidden away in a cliff cave for eons of time, she decided to go for a walk. Because of the very nature of the dream, she dared not speak to Marisol, her mother, who would instantly become alarmed. Marisol was superstitious. This dream would make her sleepwalk. Morgana's father would laugh at her, saying it was just a silly dream that needed to be purged from her mind. But, Morgana had felt the power of the dream. She believed that dreams were omens, future predictions that needed analyzing and understanding.

She dressed quickly, deciding that a long walk would help. Downstairs in the kitchen she hastily grabbed her coat and left the house.

She followed the main drive leading to the canyon road. As she walked, she failed to notice the water-filled arroyos, the rain-drenched limestone walls or the rushing waters that splashed down the tall granite outcropping. The dark clouds overhead thundered and rattled, allowing drops of rain to sprinkle upon her face. She quickly turned up the collar of her jacket, then realized that she'd walked at least four miles up the canyon road. And now a storm was brewing. She hastily wiped her eyes and glanced up at the grey sky and swirling dark clouds, then at the giant Sangre de Cristo peaks.

"Majestic peak! Speak to me!" she cried as she stood on the edge of a high cliff, hoping that the mountain would vibrate to answer her call.

For long moments she stood praying to Earth Woman, seeking harmony and peace. Father Wind tore at her hair tangling it into a hundred knots; yet, she stood braced against the cliff. She loved the mountains which she understood to be deities. Isadora told her that the mountains were homes of the Gods while the hogans were the homes of the Navajo people. Morgana believed this without question. She felt the power of the mountain each time she pulled clay from it. And, she loved the land. Like her father, she had no doubts about the land; but for life, there were no easy answers.

"I will go see Isadora soon," she decided. "She will chant for me. She will guide me through the shadows of these threatening dreams."

As she walked, she thought of her home. The ranch house was situated two miles from the main highway and made of natural stones and boulders that purposely blended in with the arid mountains. She loved the elevated patio which served as the main entrance to the house. It consisted of Spanish tiles set on a large slab. The patio led to ornate Spanish doors. Tiny steps, wide enough for four people to walk up them at once, provided easy access to the patio. From this patio one could see the varied plateau that graced the ranch. As a young girl, she had dreamt that this would be the spot where she would fall madly in love. Dreams of love, she quickly decided, were good for young women. Dreams of terror were altogether another thing.

The sound of a vehicle approaching drove her to near panic. She moved closer to the base of the high cliff. The vehicle's brakes screeched. She glanced back, recognizing her father. "Father!" She frantically waved her arms to greet him.

The vehicle pulled to a quick stop and her father rolled down the window of his pickup. "*¡Hola!* What's the matter with you? Walking in the rain like you don't have any sense!" he stated in concern.

She hurried around the front of the truck and climbed inside. "Father, I'm so glad to see you!" She shivered in her wet clothes, but did not hesitate to reach over and affectionately pat his arm.

"What's wrong, *hija*? Why aren't you home?" he asked softly as he guided the truck slowly down the curves of the canyon road.

"The dreams. They're back again. I thought I'd outgrown them, but obviously that's not the case."

He nodded that he understood. "So, you see more trouble?"

"I guess so, but who really knows. Let's go home. I'm soaked." After making herself more comfortable she asked, "Where have you been?"

"In Santa Fe. Your mother needed a few things. At the farmer's market, I sold the eggs and hot peppers. Got a good price for them, too." He winked. "Do you need any money?" he asked.

She shook her head. "No, and neither do you. You've got the profits from the cattle and I've got my pottery money. Mother has her weaving, so we've got everything we need."

He chuckled. "No, I still don't have a grandson."

"Forget that, Father. For a while anyway. What I'd like to talk about is your taking it easy this coming winter."

Frank Cruz held up his hand to stop her nagging. "Listen, if a man quits working and starts taking it easy, he gets old fast. I'm like a *pistola*, a gun, which has to be constantly oiled. Work keeps me fit. See, not an ounce of fat on this old body."

She sighed helplessly. "Father! When are you going to let me help around the ranch? I can't do pottery all my life. What if something should happen to you?"

He shook his finger at her. "You stick to your pottery and I'll stick to my ranching. People pay lots of money for your pottery. Pottery making takes talent. Cattle and a few chickens don't need any special talent to raise."

"Yes, but you're not getting any younger," she argued.

"I'm fine." He tapped his forehead. "I've got tons of good luck, *la buena suerte*! It all started the day I met your mother. What a day! I've told you about that day, haven't I?"

"Yes, Father. I know all about that day," she sighed.

The chilly twilight cast a grey hue against the sides of the stone ranch house as father and daughter walked up the steps into their home.

As they entered the large kitchen, Marisol quickly looked at her only daughter. "What happened to you?" She turned an accusing glance at her husband. "Old man, didn't you take care of her?"

Morgana stared at her mother, feeling that her mother would always look upon her as a little girl. "Father and I met on the highway." Morgana retreated to her room upstairs, to the luxury of a steamy shower.

After dinner, in her favorite room in the house, Morgana sat hypnotized by the blue and orange colors created by the blazing fire on a chilly night. She sighed, adjusted the caftan over her legs, then glanced over at her parents who were seated on the sofa. Her father was reading, and her mother was sewing, both absorbed in their own thoughts. Yet, she could swear they were carrying on their own silent conversation.

She continued to study them from lowered lashes, feeling as if she were spying on their happiness. Her parents glowed with a deep sense of inner peace and a willing acceptance of each other. Still, she felt life had short-changed them by not blessing them with more children.

"Morgana," her mother said, "tomorrow is Saturday. Would you like to go shopping with me in Santa Fe?"

"No, Mother, I think I'll help father do some ranching." She saw her father glance at her from over the pages of his book.

"That sounds like a good idea," added Marisol, not daring to look up from her sewing, for she could visualize the grim displeased expression on her husband's face.

"*¡Mujeres!* Women!" snapped Cruz as he glanced angrily at his wife, then quickly rose. "Women go shopping. They don't do ranching! Ranching is my business!" He rose, then walked to his desk, rattled some papers, pulled out a chair and within minutes was deeply absorbed in his project.

Morgana swore she heard her mother sigh in relief. She glanced back at her father. Her mother was right, she thought. He had a place for everything, even women.

Morgana's father preferred to call his wife Marisol. Marisol, my love, do this, do whatever I ask. Poor Mother, thought Morgana. She complies with whatever my father desires and with whatever I desire over all other things.

Morgana placed the cool glass of cider against her cheek and shifted her gaze from one object to another within the spacious den. The hand-hewn fireplace covered an entire wall. Her father told her it was built to accommodate any emergency and she knew visitors were always overwhelmed by its ruggedness. In bygone days the fireplace served as a stove, an oven, a source of heat to ward off the cold winters. Later, it was used as a barbecue pit. Her father truly admired versatility in all things around him. Why then, she wondered, does he not allow me to learn to operate the ranch? He probably thinks he's going to be around forever.

On the opposite wall hung a handwoven tapestry, Morgana's mother's pride and joy. Marisol was a full-blooded Navajo, with olive skin, black eyes and straight black hair, one layer of which was cut level with her chin. The other fell freely down her back.

Morgana looked up at the tapestry which had taken Marisol five years to weave. Marisol would never part with it, not even for thousands of dollars. She had turned down many offers over the years, even some very tempting ones. Everyone knew that upon her death the woven treasure would be left to her daughter.

The scene interwoven in the tapestry had always puzzled Morgana. As a child, she had sat and gazed at it trying to analyze its meaning. It was as if the whole scene were a gigantic jig-saw puzzle in which a solitary piece held the story that related to everything in Marisol's life.

Morgana flung the blanket off her legs and rose. She walked over to the tapestry and stood examining the magnificent brown, rust and gold threads. Silently, she marveled at her mother's weaving talent. Morgana was very proud that this masterpiece would be hers someday, for deep down inside her soul she realized that it stood for everything that her mother believed in and loved. Morgana had come to believe that the scene described Marisol's ancestral line, the High Plains clan.

On the left side of the tapestry stood a tall, slim muscular Indian who wore a headband with feathers of many colors representing his high tribal status. A bright sun was centered in the middle of the picture. The Indian, who Morgana believed was a chief, was standing on a high rocky cliff holding a sharp spear in his left hand and his right hand held a single rose. A silver pendant hung from his neck. In the center of the pendant was an eagle cast in silver threads. The young chief's loin cloth was of jade. Strong sturdy legs supported his body and prevented him from falling into the river.

The river was turbulent and its foaming gave Morgana the impression that it was flowing into the room where she stood. She thoughtfully ran her hand over the blue, gray and deep aqua threads that eerily created the force of nature. The wind and the mountains were familiar to her, but she had never encountered such angry waters in her daily life.

The woman woven onto the right side of the mural was young and her beauty was of a tender quality. She wore a blue headband which kept her long black hair from streaming into her face. Her only imperfection was a bold white streak of hair that marked her left side. The tribe would have said that she was marked by the evil spirit and would have treated her roughly.

Her robe was of a rich cream color. A sash made of velvet brown threads hung from her slender waist. She had neither feathers nor beads and wore no sandals on her feet. Perhaps, thought Morgana, she did not need them. Perhaps, she could walk on air, or float, for she was majestic enough. She wore no identifying jewelry, but her sculptured arm was outstretched as if pleading to the young chief to come to her. Her grayish-black eyes reflected sadness. In the tree directly behind her were birds of varied colors. She carried a basket of orange and gold wild flowers, a few of which had fallen to her feet.

Morgana thought there was no peace depicted in this one moment. Yes, there was love, but it was a sad, regretful love. She glanced over at her mother and wondered why Marisol had never wanted to explain the story behind the tapestry even though she had asked endless questions. One day, she promised herself, she would find out the mystery.

Her father rose and bade them good-night. He kissed Morgana, then Marisol, on the cheek and disappeared down the hallway and upstairs. Marisol's gaze followed her husband until he was no longer in sight. Her deep black eyes found those of her daughter's. For a brief moment, Morgana felt like inquiring about the tapestry once again, but before she could ask, her mother said, "I'm going to bed, too."

Marisol gently folded her yarn, closed her thread box and arose. Morgana got up too and gently kissed her mother on the cheek. Then she watched her mother leave the room.

Marisol would always do what Morgana's father asked. Morgana knew that for a fact. The Navajo women were trained in that way and for this reason she could not be like her mother. She had been places her mother never dreamed existed. Places that would have shocked her mother. Morgana was more like her Mexican father—a little too bold and brassy for her own good, and she enjoyed challenging him. Someday, her father would let her learn about ranching, and she was determined to force his hand very soon.

♡   ♡   ♡

The next morning Morgana awoke and glanced at her clock. She lay in bed a moment, blessing her spirit father for letting her have a dreamless night. She pushed aside the blankets and went to the bathroom. There, she brushed her hair before pulling it back at her neck and tying it with a bright pink ribbon, her favorite color. Isadora had told her that, for the Navajo, pink was symbolic of the power of the celestial worlds. It was the color that blends with the heavenly sunsets and the light blue color of the daytime sky. "For you to love the color pink is a good sign. You are indeed blessed," Isadora had said joyously. "For *disqs*, as the color is called in Navajo, is where Pink Thunder lives, in the Land-beyond-the-Sky. With his trail, Pink Thunder streaks the sky in rose pink."

Morgana smiled thinking of old Isadora; then she finished dressing and quietly left her room. Marisol was not in the kitchen when Morgana passed, and Morgana sighed with relief. Her mother would have insisted on her having breakfast before going to her work shed.

Today, Morgana planned on firing a very special vase and she wanted to get started early. As quietly as she could, she opened the back door, then hurried in the direction of her workshop which was situated on a remote plateau her father had sectioned off from the rest of the property. As she followed the well worn path, she glanced about in the distance searching for her father. Not seeing him, she decided he must be working inside the barn.

She pulled out her keys and unlocked the door of the workroom. Once inside, she opened the window and proceeded immediately to the back of the hut and outside to her firing pit. This she loaded with a delicately carved Navajo Wedding Vase, the project she had been working on for the last few months. Now she decided to experiment with the glazes, hoping to achieve a complicated hue of black, streaked with metallic luster. With the glazes she hoped to create the image of rings encircling the base of the vase. Achieving the desired effect would depend on her timing while the vase was fired in the pit. If all turned out as she hoped, she'd get a nice price from Bo, her dealer.

She bent over the side of the pit and began shoveling layers of special earth mixed with cow manure and coals until her piece was entirely covered. Nasty work, she thought, but the resulting masterpiece was well worth all her efforts. The glaze at the top should remain lustrous and smooth enough so that the lips of the bride and groom would shiver with awe when they tasted the blessed wine inside. The vase would be astonishing and as priceless as her mother's tapestry. "Yes," she said, "this piece is created for a very special person." Perhaps a prince or queen would buy the piece for their collection. The thought thrilled her. She'd best settle for an ordinary collector to purchase her masterpiece, she quickly decided. Morgana worked steadily until the late afternoon. Then, she decided to leave the intricate firing until early the next morning.

Chapter 2

In the early dawn, Morgana rose and went to her workshop. It was time to fire her wedding vase. With a thick poking iron she stirred the edges of the pit and carefully arranged the vase in its center. She took a match, lit it, and carefully shoveled cold ashes over the vase to serve as a protective outer coating. As the fire slowly grew, she listened for popping noises, often created when pots cracked as the intensity of the fire grew.

She was afraid she'd made the base too thin, but she wanted a delicate piece and she had searched hard for the clay in the high altitudes of the Sandía Mountains. Yet she knew that all her hours of effort to create the piece could be ruined by a single misfire. She had to keep the fire slightly cooler than normal, thereby sacrificing a bit of hardness to gain a deeper black finish. She stirred the mixture once more, then sat cross-legged before the pit, pulling the loose threads at the knees of her old jeans.

Then she adjusted a blanket around her shoulders to ward off the cool morning air.

This wedding vase would be beautiful. It would be admired and used by a bride and groom who had eyes only for each other. Then it would be passed around to all the family members so that they too would partake of the sacred wine. The men would drink out of the spout that bore the emblem of feathers and the women would drink from the symbol of the hummingbird. "It will be a gorgeous piece," she stated as she rocked in slow rhythm to a chant that escaped her lips:

> "Oh, Sacred Fire, allow my art to flow,
> Oh, White Spirit, allow a soul to behold
> the beauty I've dedicated to you.
> Mother Earth, allow your gift of clay to glow
> With gold and black and smiles of admiration,
> For what I take from you
> I give to humankind.

She chanted with eyes closed and with arms folded across her breasts. "It will be good!" she exclaimed. The chill of the wind encircled her. She inhaled deeply, for this was her time alone. After a while she felt cold and moved closer to the pit, seeking its warmth. Her spirit was set free to roam

14

through the dark ashes of the pit, sending a thrill of feelings into her delicate vase.

While stroking the pit every hour or so, she hummed an Indian lullaby, allowing the quiet of the plateau to surround her. She soon became drowsy due to the aroma of the smoke and the warm flames that escaped the pit and she allowed her head to fall forward as total relaxation began to overtake her.

It was the whisper of her name that aroused her.

"Morgana. Ho, Morgana! Listen to me! It is time!"

She slowly lifted her head and glanced around the area. She saw nothing, even though she recognized the voice. Sitting straight-backed and cross-legged, she listened. Then she heard the wind hiss her mentor's name: "ISADORA, ISADORA!"

Alarmed, Morgana rose and searched the early morning sky. She saw nothing, yet she had heard Isadora call her. She stirred the flameless pit carefully, then glanced apprehensively at her watch. In another hour or so the firing should be completed. Then, she would definitely seek out Isadora. She bent on her knees to study the cooling ashes. The outer layer was almost gray. She fetched her pitchfork and slowly removed the outside stones, shoving them to the outer edges of the pit. Slowly she pulled away the chicken wire that protected the vase. Fifteen minutes were needed to allow it to cool; then she would be able to determine if her prayers were answered and if her vase was as beautiful as she hoped it would be.

After checking her watch, she knelt beside the pit and blew at the ashes that coated her vase. The ashes scattered in all directions, allowing her to peek at the deep blue-black vase.

"Yes," she cried happily. She reached for her pitchfork and carefully lifted the piece. She was pleased, more so than she'd dared hope. The vase was hot. Morgana picked it up with prongs and moved to her studio where, as carefully as she could, she placed the vase on a soft flame-proof pad. At this stage, she did not want to risk scratching the finish, so she took a soft brush and dusted the bottom section. "You are beautiful!" she said to the vase as she clapped her hands happily.

She left the vase to cool and ran to the house to change before going out to look for Isadora. She quickly put on clean jeans and a turquoise sweater and fastened a silver concho belt around her waist. Then she arranged her turquoise and crystal pendant around her neck.

Downstairs she found her mother in her weaving room. "Mama, I'm going up to the mountain to see Isadora."

Marisol cast her a serious glance. "Has anything happened?

"Yes. While at my pit, I heard Isadora calling me by way of the wind."

Marisol stepped off the foot pedals of the loom and put down the thread. "She may be ill."

"She is old, Mama. I am ashamed that I have not visited her more often. I shall drive up to her hogan to see if she is all right." Morgana turned to leave.

"Wait, daughter. Perhaps I should go too."

Morgana stopped at the door. "It's not necessary, Mother. I'll tell you about her when I return."

Marisol nodded. "Then take her some money. She may need some." Marisol disappeared through a draped opening that led to her bedroom then quickly returned. "Give this to Isadora and bid her hello. You be careful. Watch the road for the evil coyote. Are you carrying your protection in the pouch? And the crystal that Isadora gave you with her blessing? Both have magic powers."

"I have the pouch tucked in the pocket of my jeans."

Marisol followed Morgana downstairs to the front door. "Call me if you need help. I will follow immediately."

"Yes, Mother." Morgana reached the white jeep, threw in her bag and drove out the two miles to the highway, then headed north, seeking the familiar six-sided hogan that belonged to Isadora.

There were few cars on the highway and Morgana was able to travel fast. She glanced at her watch and realized it would be an hour or more before she reached Isadora. She laughed to herself remembering the warnings about coyotes her mother always gave her when she headed north to Navajo country or toward the reservation. Real coyotes run holding their tails outstretched her mother had warned. But, when a witch has transformed itself into a coyote, the poor animal's tail hangs straight down as if it were ashamed of itself. Morgana laughed, then stroked the crystal.

Like Morgana's mother, Isadora believed in the power of black medicine. She insisted that for every spell there was a remedy for a price to pay later on. Isadora had been her teacher—the master who taught her the secrets of the clay and how to make the pottery. A long time ago, Marisol had taken Morgana to Isadora when Morgana decided pottery would be her craft. She had studied and stayed with Isadora on weekends, learning all the pottery secrets the woman possessed. She had also learned about the intricate Navajo teaching of First Man, First Woman and Coyote who have the responsibility for introducing magical powers into the world.

Morgana shivered because she knew she'd never be able to work with any of the magical spells. She felt a definite inner resistance to learning about the art of magic. But, she'd learned to respect the powers Isadora taught her about spells and their meanings.

On sensing the child's fear, Isadora had given Morgana the pouch for her twelfth birthday. "This is protection for you. All it contains is cornmeal mixed with the gall of an eagle, a special mixture I've concocted especially for you. Its protection will last a lifetime."

Morgana accepted the gift though at the time she did not fully understand its purpose. She had not wanted to hurt Isadora's feeling by refusing the ugly pouch which consisted of an old leather piece roughly laced together. On it was a small flap where Isadora attached a safety pin and fastened it to the hem of Morgana's skirt.

"That's all you have to do," explained Isadora. "You must never open the pouch, for there is no need for that."

"I understand," replied Morgana. "I will wear it forever."

Isadora smiled. "Just don't tell anyone you're wearing it," she advised.

"Not even mother?" Morgana had exclaimed, as she looked out of the doorway of the hogan.

Isadora smiled. "Yes, you may tell your mother."

"Good!" replied Morgana. "I know she'll be pleased."

Morgana shook away her thoughts of the past and glanced down at her watch. In another fifteen minutes she'd arrive at Isadora's.

The deserted highway curved sharply. Morgana slowed down to exit onto a dirt road. From this point the ride would be bumpy and she would have to drive carefully. She realized she should have hitched La Luna, her horse, to the jeep so that she could travel uphill faster, but she'd been in a big hurry and didn't think of it when she left home. Since the last rain, the holes in the road had become deeper and they were still mud-filled. Morgana glanced at her watch. It was almost high noon. She shifted gears and continued at a faster pace aware that she might do damage to the jeep. She softly cursed the road, then instinctively, she knew she must hurry as her hand reached down to touch the crystal for encouragement. She immediately began to rub the crystal as if it were a worry rock. In the past, the crystal always eased her stress and served as a comfort to her, but today, it merely seemed to dampen her spirits.

Morgana tried to concentrate on her driving, but found herself instead thinking about the day she had turned sixteen. She remembered that on that day Isadora had said, "Morgana, I have something for you. The last gift you shall receive from me."

"Isadora," Morgana had said, "you have taught me so much. You do not need to give me a gift."

The old woman had sat on a bear rug in her hogan, untangling the pigtail of her silver-white hair and replaiting it. "You have now mastered the gift of clay. You know all that I know of shaping and painting, and where to find the pigments to make paints and pottery. Now, you are responsible to Mother Earth for what you design and produce from her. So, do not get greedy. You have talent and a feel for the soul of the clay. You will do well. Should you have a change of heart and want another profession, remember the Indian school needs teachers to train their young ones. You will be sorely needed should you decide to follow that path. Now, open my gift to you."

Morgana had slowly unrolled a small leather pouch. "Oh, a crystal! How beautiful, Isadora." She had held up the crystal piece to examine it in the light and saw that it was shaped like an thick arrow. As she examined it, she had exclaimed, "I see a face in it, Isadora!"

The old woman had smiled. "You are alert. Yes, it is the Great Father spirit. He who says 'Ho!' which means 'Hear Me!' He will protect you." She had gently stroked the girl's hair. "Remember that crystals are used in many Navajo ceremonies. A crystal signifies 'Stone-through-which-light-beams,' and it symbolizes fire, especially when used with our prayersticks which contain tobacco." She had smiled like a child again. "An ancient story tells us that at the beginning of creation a crystal was put on the tongue of every person so that everything said would come true. I, myself, put small chip crystals in my pollen bags. You see, the pollen represents well-being while the crystal represents the words that make the prayer come true."

"Isadora, I shall always remember all these things." Morgana had hugged the old woman.

Chapter 3

The memories of all the encounters she and Isadora shared for many years suddenly evaporated. Morgana screamed as the tires of the jeep hit a deep rut which she'd mistaken for a puddle of water. She released the steering wheel, then got out to inspect the damage. "Oh, my!" she cried when she saw the wheel submerged in mud. To get help was next to impossible.

She took her bag, locked the jeep and trudged up the wet path as fast as she could. "I should have brought La Luna!" She scolded herself once again for not bringing her pinto. Then she climbed upward as rapidly as she could, not caring that mud covered her boots, not sensing the drizzle that fell lightly upon her head.

She glanced up from the path and could see the bend leading to Isadora's hogan. The rain had soaked her clothes completely; yet, she trudged onward somehow knowing that time was of the essence. As she reached the bend, she saw smoke seeping out of the tip of Isadora's hogan and allowed herself a smile. Maybe all her fear was just in her imagination. Isadora might be waiting for her in her usual cross-legged position, smoking her ancient, worn out corn-husk pipe. But suddenly Morgana tripped and fell. Mud covered her arms up to her elbows. She rose, shook herself, then ran all the faster crying—"Isadora! Isadora! Isadora!"

From out of a clump of cedar trees a man emerged before her. He was tall and muscular, with arms crossed over his chest. A bear skin protected him from the rain. His brown boots were mud-covered as were his jeans. Morgana noticed his silver beltbuckle with a turquoise eagle whose ebony eyes appeared angry and rebellious. The man seized her tightly by the arm. "Quiet, woman! Isadora is to meet her maker!"

His hostility enraged Morgana. "I am Morgana Cruz. Isadora calls me!"

"Yes," he said and quickly moved to her side, still holding her elbow as he calmly walked beside her.

His authoritative manner angered Morgana as she glanced up at the man. His jaw was sharp and his nose angled sharply downward. His lips were full and slightly parted. "Who are you?" she asked, looking into his fierce eyes.

"I am Eagle Eyes. Others call me Rusty."

Morgana felt like laughing, but dared not. Rusty, she was sure, would not appreciate it. His Anglo name was not common among the Indians, she thought, and he did not appear to be friendly.

They reached the hogan where another man waited near the opening. He pulled open the door and let Morgana pass.

Isadora lay on her back, encircled by steaming bricks which were keeping her warm. Morgana noticed that Isadora was lying on top of a decorative blanket that Marisol had woven. A thick bear skin covered the old woman. The silver white hair that Morgana had seen Isadora braid countless times fanned out from beneath her head. In the hogan Morgana recognized another person—the Holy Man. She glanced at him, then knelt close to Isadora. Cautiously, she reached out and touched her old master's skin. It was slick and hot.

Isadora, my teacher, speak to me," Morgana whispered into her ear. "I came as quickly as I could." She smoothed the old woman's hair and glanced nervously at the Holy Man who was seriously studying her. She knew she must be careful not to displease him.

Isadora moved her head toward Morgana. She grasped a thick handful of Morgana's hair as if to prove to herself that Morgana was really there. "My girl. I have missed you." She coughed. The cough wracked through her entire body. Isadora waited a moment for the pain to subside. Then she looked up at Morgana with eyes that soon filled with tears. "I have waited for you to come. I prayed that I be allowed to see you once more before my time arrived. I know that you are not my blood, but I love you as my only daughter. If I could have one last wish it would be that you remain happy for all the time you have left upon Mother Earth." Isadora moved her hand from beneath the bearskin, wanting to draw Morgana near to her. "Listen to your dreams, my girl, even though they are dark and ugly at times. Protect yourself at all times, for you are generous, and evil people are very cruel and may take advantage of you. Keep your soul true. Hear me, child."

"Isadora," Morgana begged, paying no attention to what the old woman had said, "let me bring a doctor from below."

"No!" objected the old woman as she tightly grabbed Morgana's arm. "Nothing can prevent Fate from doing what it should. I accept this and the blessings Fate brings." She gently caressed Morgana's cheek. "I promise you that I will watch over you from the highest mountains. I will help you in ways you know nothing about. I will be strong when you are weak. You will live in my heart forever."

"But Isadora!" Morgana objected, noticing that as she stared into her master's eyes that she was seeing spinning tunnels. Instantly, Morgana knew that to make the transition to the spirit world Isadora's soul must pass through those same tunnels. Morgana could not prevent a sob.

"Isadora," she whispered softly, "don't cross over. Fight it. I know you are powerful, more so than the Medicine Man. Fight it, Isadora!"

The Holy Man glanced at her as he rose, then began chanting as he danced around the two grief-striken women. Each time he circled them he looked coldly at Morgana as if wanting her thrown out of the hogan.

"I want you to stay with me, my daughter, until I reach the spirit world." Isadora's bone-thin arms reached out and encircled Morgana's head to draw her closer. "Of all things on Mother Earth, I shall miss you and my Eagle the most."

Morgana wept quietly as she rocked the old woman back and forth. "I love you Isadora. Hear me." Suddenly, Isadora gasped. Morgana knew that Isadora no longer breathed; yet, she did not let her go. Kneeling near her teacher, Morgana sang in a broken whispery voice the Indian lullaby of farewell that Isadora had taught her many years before.

She remained motionless, weeping bitterly into Isadora's thin shoulder until the Holy Man touched her head. Then she carefully laid Isadora back onto the blanket and put the old woman's arms underneath the bearskin. Morgana then sat back on her knees.

She was not aware of how long she sat there with Isadora's body. Her quivering chin dropped upon her chest as she retraced all the fond memories she had of Isadora. She remembered the many hills they'd climbed in search of red clay, the aching hands they had both blistered, the laughter they had shared, the love, and the many secrets they talked of during those precious times. Isadora had indeed been like a grandmother to Morgana.

Her throbbing knees made her painfully aware of the time that had elapsed since Isadora had stopped breathing. She glanced across the low burning fire and met the sharp critical gaze of the stranger who called himself Eagle Eyes. His eyes were painted in the traditional red and black circles of mourning and never wavered as he searched every inch of her body.

She sensed that he knew her deepest secrets. His penetrating eyes were red-brown with golden flecks as if the sun were reflected in them. As of yet, he had not spoken a word. Could he be the diviner she wondered? She glanced around the hogan looking for the Holy Man, then realized he was no longer present. Her gaze returned to the man with the piercing eyes who must certainly be the diviner, the expert who would know the rules and laws of the Navajo customs. The diviner was of a higher position within the tribal structure than the Medicine Man and according to tribal customs it was he who instructed the Medicine Man as to which chant to use.

Morgana trembled under his bold stare. Still, she dared not speak until he spoke first, and it was apparent that he would not do so. Her gaze fell upon Isadora's peaceful face. Morgana shifted her weight from her knees, then reached down to touch Isadora's face, but as she did so, a decorated staff, filled with colorful black and red feathers, fell sharply against her wrist. The man called Eagle Eyes gently pried Morgana's hand away from Isadora's body.

"Do not touch her until it is time for cleansing," he said as he slowly laid the staff to his right side.

Morgana's eyes flashed with anger. "Tell me of your relationship to my teacher, Isadora."

"She was also my teacher," Eagle Eyes stated, and in a much softer voice continued, "She was my teacher years before you came to her and during your apprenticeship also."

He shows no emotion, she thought, as he gazed upon the old woman's face. Morgana guessed that he was no more than five or six years older than she was and wondered why Isadora had never spoken of him. She rose, then said, "I must inform my mother of Isadora's death."

"No!" declared Eagle Eyes as he instantly rose. "Isadora has chosen you and me to arrange for her burial in the sacred grounds."

Morgana shook her head. "That cannot be, for I am half-clan. I cannot enter the sacred grounds. I will get mother. She is full blood." She walked around the fire toward the entrance of the hogan, but he shot forward and blocked her way. "You are not permitted to leave!" he stated fiercely.

Morgana's heart raced in fear as she gazed upon his throat and chin, then slowly at his eyes. Don't be afraid of this man, she told herself several times before she was able to ask, "What is it you wish?" She moved her eyes slowly downcast, hoping he did not sense her fear.

He reached out and lifted a lock of her long hair and carefully brought it to his lips and then to his nose to smell.

She gasped in surprise and bolted back, away from him.

He released her hair and stood staring at her before he commanded, "You will clean and dress Isadora in her finest. You will not leave this hogan. It is commanded. Do you understand?" He reached out, pulled her to him, and held her tight against his chest before he boldly added, "You will also clean yourself. It is required that you be pure. I will send clothes for you to wear. And again I warn you ... do not try to leave this hogan for fear of death."

She felt his strong arms, his firm chest and the racing of his heart. His penetrating stare unnerved her. The tone of his voice signified that he meant every word he said. His face was painted with red chee, a special pigment, drawn in a ceremonial line across his cheek bone and over his nose. Red, the color of danger, the color of war and sorcery. Red if used in combination with the black hue was deadly. Suddenly, she felt faint and extremely weak against the solid body of this man called Eagle Eyes who also bore the name of Rusty.

Just as quickly as he had grabbed her, he let her go and she fell to the floor of the hogan, crumpled like a rag doll. She rolled over to lash out at him, but he'd already disappeared through the doorway of the hogan.

Morgana approached the entrance of the hogan and angrily opened the door. A man who stood guard at the entrance of the hogan stared at her. He took hold of the door and quickly pulled it closed, thus preventing Morgana from seeing outside. Morgana felt herself very much a captive now. Slowly, she turned back to Isadora as desperation pierced her heart.

"Isadora, my teacher, what shall I do now?" she questioned. "This Eagle Eyes whom I fear so much, who is he? Why does he think he can command me the way he does? What should I do to keep him from hurting me?"

Chapter 4

According to tribal custom, they would take Isadora to the sacred burial grounds before nightfall. Morgana glanced at the rolled up leather bundle in the corner of the hogan which contained the beaded dress Isadora had prepared for her burial. She took the bundle and gently unrolled it. The dress was made of the finest soft leather, dyed almost gray blue and beaded in coral, black, turquoise and silver. The front of the dress had a star filled in with tiny yellow beads, one of the brilliant sacred colors of the Navajo which represented the power of reproduction and growth. Isadora no longer could develop on Mother Earth, but in the spirit world she would be adorned with strong powers more defined than those she used on earth.

Morgana's tears fell upon the soft leather and she quickly wiped them away. Unable to contain her fears and the uncertainties of the situation, she fell to her knees crying.

Another woman entered the hogan with water and cloth. She glanced at Morgana, then set the water and cloth near Isadora's body. "I am Bittersweet. You are very pretty, as they say. You must hurry, the sun falls. Eagle Eyes will return soon and all must be ready."

Morgana glanced up at her questioningly, then said, "I do not know what to say ... or what to do."

Bittersweet, who seemed to be around eighteen, smiled. "Cleanse your Master first, anoint her body with oil, then dress her. I shall bring her feathers." Quietly she left the hogan.

Morgana rose and slowly moved to where Isadora's body lay. Still wishing her mother was with her, she began to sponge Isadora tenderly from the tip of her head to her toes. She wept as she removed all traces of ointment the medicine man had used, then proceeded to comb and braid Isadora's silky silver hair with colorful ribbons.

Isadora lay splendidly dressed and ready for burial when Bittersweet arrived with Isadora's headdress of white feathers. Morgana took the headdress from the young woman, then carefully arranged it on Isadora's head. She is as beautiful in death as she was in life, thought Morgana as she knelt by Isadora's side, faintly aware that Bittersweet was waiting near the entrance of the hogan.

After several moments, Bittersweet's hand touched Morgana's shoulder. "You must dress. Eagle Eyes has instructed me to dress you."

"I can dress myself," muttered Morgana, refusing to take her eyes away from Isadora.

"You do not understand," the girl explained, "I must dress you now. You fulfilled your duty to her. Now, you shall be treated like an Indian princess."

Morgana raised her hand high in objection. "I really don't care about the details of the ceremony. Nor do I understand them, for I am half-breed. As far as I'm concerned Isadora has departed!"

"You are exhausted, as expected, but Eagle Eyes waits patiently as do the others. We must hurry." Without waiting any longer, Bittersweet removed Morgana's outer clothes carefully and rolled them into a bundle which she placed in a basket. She turned slightly to the side and patiently waited for Morgana to remove the rest of her clothing. "Now, I have to bathe you, quickly, too, for all thunder will break loose if Eagle Eyes is not pleased."

The water she used to bathe Morgana felt cool and refreshing, making Morgana feel tired and sleepy. She took a brush and combed Morgana's hair, then braided only the sides over her ears, adding ribbons of white. The back of Morgana's hair was left to fall down to her waist.

Bittersweet whispered, "Hold your arms out and I shall slip the dress over them."

Morgana looked at a white leather shift. It was cut simply; yet, the soft white leather felt elegant to Morgana's touch. The turquoise beads were colorful, placed in the leather fringe that served as a collar and hung from the sleeves. "It's a maiden's dress. Whose is it?"

"Yours," Bittersweet responded. "Isadora made it for you. See, your soft boots have silver." She pointed out the intricate threadwork and silver stars on the white leather boots which came to just below her knees.

"Yes, they are lovely," Morgana said, bowing her head slightly. "But, I don't understand how all this came to be?"

"It is not meant to be understood, but to be accepted. It is the Navajo way." Bittersweet pulled the dress over Morgana's head. "Eagle Eyes knows all things ... that is to say, he sees things. I believe it scares him," she added as she carefully placed each boot on Morgana's feet, then stepped away to survey her work.

"It seems you know him well."

Bittersweet smiled and added, "He is of my clan." After she finished with the dress she said, "I think he will be pleased." She brought a clay mug and held it out to Morgana. "Sip this, it will refresh and nourish you."

Morgana took it, realizing that she was very thirsty. "Is there magic in it?" she asked seriously before she sipped the drink that tasted like thin honey.

The girl laughed. "No, it is nectar. Quick energy. It is good." She watched Morgana sip slowly. "You are ready. But you should not leave the hogan until instructed to do so." She glanced at Morgana for a final inspection, waved gently, then opened the door of the hogan and disappeared.

Seconds later the drums began to sound so loudly that Morgana's heart skipped countless beats, and the ground beneath her feet vibrated, causing her to cover her ears with her hands. Suddenly the door opened. She stepped through and glanced up to see Eagle Eyes before her.

Eagle Eyes was dressed in full ceremonial garb. A headdress of black, white and red feathers hung down his back. The beads that adorned the leather band were of a series of eagles. Encircled on his arm was a braided leather bracelet decorated in colorful beads and feathers. His loin cloth was decorated with the symbol of the eagle.

Morgana saw a white mare adorned in feathers and a bridle. She recognized it as Isadora's. The mare towed a travois. Colorful feathers decorated the two poles that dragged behind the mare and the net that secured the two poles was decorated with a colorful bed of sweetgrass and wildflowers. Eagle Eyes took the reins and moved the horse closer to Morgana. The horse, Morgana noticed, seemed unusually skittish.

"You must stand here," Eagle Eyes commanded.

Morgana moved opposite him so that only the horse's head separated her from Eagle Eyes. Four men entered the hogan. Morgana glanced to see members of the tribe waiting a respectable distance away. In a slow manner, the men emerged from the hogan with Isadora's body. She was covered with a sheepskin up to her waist. They gently placed Isadora on the A-shaped travois and in quick motion secured her body to the frame, then moved away.

Morgana heard Eagle Eyes say to the people, "We shall lead the horse around the hogan once, then as friends of Isadora, we shall wait as the hogan is burned to the ground."

Morgana gasped.

"You must remain quiet and obey," he ordered in a whisper.

The horse snorted and shook his head as if objecting to the whole ceremony. Morgana held the bridle in her right hand while Eagle Eyes held the bridle on the opposite side with his left hand.

They moved slowly forward with Morgana walking on the inside and Eagle Eyes on the outside of the circle. For this Morgana was thankful, as it allowed her some privacy from the watchful eyes of the people.

Try as she would to hold her head proudly, she could not. Every step she took was in unison with the roll of the drums which added to the pounding that never ceased inside her head. She stumbled, but clutched the bridle tightly.

Moments passed before she realized that it was his hand that steadied her and prevented her from falling. He uttered not a word of encouragement. The horse snorted and looked at her as if sensing her uneasiness. She placed her head gently against the soft white coat of the mare who slowed her pace in an effort to comfort Morgana.

When they had completed the full circle, she stood facing the entrance to the hogan. Eagle Eyes moved toward the hogan, as did the four other men representing the four corners of the earth—the North, the South, the East and the West. Eagle Eyes stood at the entrance reciting a chant unknown to Morgana. She glanced at Isadora, seeking the kind of courage only the old woman could give her.

Torches were lit. Morgana gasped and moved forward to stop the burning. The horse stomped restlessly as Morgana cried out, "Stop! Stop! This is insane!"

She could not prevent the men from setting fire to the hogan that had been Isadora's and it took but a moment for the flames to reach as high as the hogan's tip. Morgana stood, hands covering her mouth to prevent a scream as the black smoke curled high into the sky.

Her sobs cried out, her heart and her eyes not accepting the Navajo custom of annihilation of all possessions. She remembered Isadora had told her that this cleansing of material possessions was necessary so that the spirit of these items could join the spirit of the deceased.

Suddenly Eagle Eyes clutched her wrist tightly.

She saw that he was staring at Isadora's horse. "Not the mare!" she screamed as she struggled against Eagle Eyes. "The mare is innocent! She hasn't done anything! This is crazy!" Eagle Eyes held Morgana by her waist as she fought with all her strength. With the other hand he held his rifle.

"No!" she sobbed, then shrieked as the sound of the fired rifle pierced the white mare's skull as sharply as it pierced her heart. Morgana collapsed unconscious—stunned by the ritual she did not understand—no longer caring, no longer sensing. She was unaware that the brown stallion was now hitched to the travois and that Eagle Eyes had mounted the stallion, nor did she sense that she was being lifted up into his arms. She did not hear his final command to the four men who represented the four regions. Eagle Eyes slowly moved the stallion, Isadora's body and the unconscious Morgana to the next site of the ancient burial ritual.

As they moved upward, higher to the tip of the sacred mountains, Eagle Eyes glanced down at Morgana's eyes in search of some movement. He rubbed her cheek with his, but she failed to stir. Her skin felt cold; he stopped and pulled out a blanket to throw around her. The blackness of the night now invaded the path, but he was not concerned. He knew the path well, as did his warrior horse. He knew what he had to do, for Isadora, his predecessor, had taught him well.

This woman of mixed blood disturbed him. She stirred him as no other woman had, not even Singing Waters for whom he had great affection. Singing Waters was the woman he thought he loved until, as Isadora had predicted, this half-breed had shaken his being, troubling him. He had laughed at Isadora saying, "It will never happen." Yet, here he was with this strange woman on his way to bury Isadora. To be alone with Morgana for four days would be difficult; yet, the ceremony had to last four days as declared by Navajo law and custom.

He moved higher up the mountain. The smell of moist cedars and the misty night air heightened his sense of oneness with nature. A feeling of purpose and peace overtook him as he approached the site for Isadora's burial.

He dismounted and carefully laid Morgana down on a blanket, then covered her securely. As he knelt over her, he ran his finger over her cheeks, her nose, and her forehead. Still, she did not stir. Her olive skin in contrast to his red rugged complexion caused him to draw away from her, but he sat by her side a moment watching the moonlight as it made her skin glow like silver in the night. She was part Mexican, he had found out. A good race, he thought, one of patience and goodness. Like his Navajos, they too, were artists in their own right.

He had seen her once before, as a child leaving Isadora's hogan. Even then she glowed with youth, eagerness, and the promise of a successful future. Her mother, as tribe gossip went, was touched in spirit. A fragile flower, Marisol had been a tribal princess who had been brutally raped by a drunk Apache warrior.

Eagle Eyes had told Isadora that the burial custom would be much too severe for someone like Morgana untrained in the Navajo way. But for some inexplicable reason Isadora remained adamant and chose him and Morgana to do the burial honors.

He glanced back at Isadora's body and wondered. What reason do you have behind all this, Isadora, he asked. I knew you well, better than even she knew you. She is only a half-breed. She has not earned the right to do the burial honor; yet, you insisted upon her. He shook his head sadly.

He rose and went to his warrior horse and unhitched the travois. He pulled the travois into a specially built cedar tepee, then turned to build a fire. Moments later, it blazed high. He moved around the fire and carefully picked Morgana up and laid her on a soft clump of cedar brush nearer to the fire. He covered her, making sure she was warm, then laid down beside her, thinking of how it tormented him to kill the horses of those deceased.

Every time he killed a magnificent beast his soul felt as though it had been submerged in a deep cold sea, but all these deeds were his duty, he had been told.

The ancient custom decreed that the belongings of the dead one must be destroyed or else the spirit of the departed person would forever come back for his or her possessions. Navajos did this to show respect, to show that the deceased was a person well loved by those who survived. Eagle Eyes did not want to think about this custom. The burial ritual was hard enough to complete and he did not need to add his own mental torment to it as well. He moved closer to Morgana and immediately fell asleep.

Morgana woke up. The owl's cry had stirred her. Her eyes saw the star-filled sky above and the silver moon, which shone so brightly. She felt she could reach out and touch them all. She became aware of Eagle Eyes beside her and she dared not move for fear of waking him. Where was she? Why did it smell so clean and powerful like the fragrance of freshly cut cedar? It seemed as if she too had died and passed to the spirit world.

She slowly turned her head to glance at him. He was handsome, but because he had killed that beautiful horse, she feared he was brutal. There was no sense to the destruction. He moaned softly. She saw that he was sleeping, but he was dreaming, crying in his sleep. She remembered the look in his eye right before he shot the horse. They were sad, yet hard. He whimpered in his sleep.

She could run away, but where would she go?

Instead, she turned to her side and covered his shoulders with part of her blanket. She studied his face—the sharp dimples, the notch under his full lips, and his angled nose. Had it been broken before, she wondered? Isadora, surely, he must be your son, she thought. The rhythm of his slow breathing caused her to drop off to sleep within a short time.

The early morning sun warmed Morgana's chilled face and woke her. She sat up quickly finding herself disoriented and confused. Her head throbbed as she searched the area for Eagle Eyes. He was not around. To her left was a small hut much like that of a beaver's mound. Through the opening she caught sight of the travois and Isadora's body.

The campfire smoldered, gently sending smoke up through the trees into the gray ever-changing clouds that were so near. The air she inhaled was thin. Perhaps this air was the reason for her discomfort. No, she decided, she simply was hungry. After all, she had slept many hours on very hard ground, something she had never done in her entire life. She sat up and listened to the birds, the occasional rustle of the trees, but she could not sense if Eagle Eyes was near enough to be watching her.

She sat next to the Isadora's body for a long while, then began pacing around the camp to keep from screaming at the top of her lungs; yet, she dared not walk off for fear of getting lost. She did not recognize any of the other mountain peaks and could not tell where these mountains were located. She knew she was still on reservation land, but where exactly were they? The top of the mountain was not flat and she found herself constantly leaning at an angle. If she'd known her location, she'd have been gone from this place long ago. But not even Eagle Eyes's horse was available for escape.

It was morning. Her mother would be worried. Surely, she must be on her way to the reservation. She would find the hogan burned to the ground, but would anyone tell her of her daughter's whereabouts?

The warrior's horse neighed and Morgana spun around to see Eagle Eyes dismounting. "I have to go!" she demanded as she rushed to him.

He ignored her, taking the blanket off the horse, then removed several pheasants which he'd strung on a strap. "We will finish with Isadora."

"I know nothing of this custom!" she screamed.

"She chose you and that is a great honor for a ... woman."

"Honor means different things to different people and it is a word that is often misused ... woman or not!"

"Look," he added in a softer voice, "I am not here to argue ethics, laws or customs. I am here to bury Isadora. So let's make a truce and get the job done in the allotted time. Then I will take you to the reservation where you will be free."

He pulled out his knife and gutted the pheasant, then started to clean it expertly, while Morgana stood silently by. "I don't suppose you know how to do this?"

"No! I don't think I'd like to learn, either!"

"Then you will be hungry by nightfall," he added.

"So, I must learn to clean the pheasant if I am to eat." She tapped her foot angrily against the ground.

He nodded as he drew his gleaming steel knife to gut the bird on which he worked. He tossed twigs upon the fire, picked up his water pouch, poured water on the bird to clean it, and then pierced a sharp twig through it after which he set it over the fire to cook.

"Are you going to clean that one?" he asked as he looked up at her from his squatting position.

"No," she stormed, then turned her back to him.

"As you like," he added. He reached over, took the pheasant and quickly cleaned it. Placing it over the fire, he said, "After I've eaten, we shall build Isadora's stand. You might as well conserve your energy. Chopping trees is hard work."

Morgana moved toward a small boulder a little distance away from him, sat on it, and looked out over the view of rugged mountains and trees. The morning sun spread its golden rays over the far reaching mountains. The breeze blew her hair in cascading directions. She sat with ankles crossed. No, she would not defeather birds or anything else! Maybe when he slept, or was away from camp, she could find some berries to eat, tiding her over during this predicament.

Eagle Eyes watched Morgana as he ate the pheasants. She was proud, but he knew how well hunger kills pride and vanity. No, he mused sadly, she's in for a rough four days. She will learn the Indian way. She will learn that when all is said and done only the soul remains. He stood up and slowly walked to the warrior horse. From his blanket, he pulled out his large ax. "Come!" he yelled, beckoning her to follow. "Follow me as best you can."

She turned to see that he was already on his way toward the thickest part of the forest. She ran fast to keep sight of him. After about twenty minutes or so, he stopped and surveyed the area. "This tree will do," he said.

She caught up with him and fell to her knees, bending over in an effort to control her frenzied heart and catch her breath. Her lungs were so belabored that she could not ask his intention.

He pulled out a knife, pointed it at her, then expertly threw it, landing it an inch from her knees. She screamed, then fell to her side quickly. "Are you crazy?" she yelled angrily.

He laughed. "Take this knife and prepare to clean small branches and twigs that might prevent the piece from being smooth." He turned his back to her and began to swing the ax against the tree. The tree soon came down and when it finally fell, he moved it close to her so that she could start to work on one end while he gave one final chop to the end which would leave the log the proper size in length.

Morgana took the carved handle of the knife in her hand with fierce determination. Yes, she would work—and work hard—just to show him that she was a very capable person. She glanced up from where she worked as he searched the perimeter for another tree. Within minutes, he had felled another tree and pulled it alongside the one Morgana now worked to complete.

"How many do we need?" she asked.

"Eight," he answered, then turned his attention back to searching for another tree.

"Eight!" she cried out. "Ridiculous!"

The task soon absorbed her entire attention. Her hands, hardened from pulling and picking clay from the country of the high sierras, now ached from the roughness and hardness of the wood. The bark chipped and scratched her up to her elbows, but she dared not stop. As she finished the first logs, she was amazed to count seven logs before her, ready to be cleaned. He reached down, pulled the cleaned one from beneath her, then left with it.

She saw that her hands were bleeding and rubbed them with leaves in hopes of relieving the ache, then sat back to rest before starting on the next log. She had no idea that the burial involved so much work. In her innocence, or ignorance, she knew not which, she believed that the stand was prepared in advance. She frowned unhappily. Why aren't Indians buried like everyone else? What else, she thought sadly, did she not know?

She worked hard, ignoring the pain, thinking of her sheltered life, her pleasant father and her quiet but sad mother. How would their burial be carried out? What if her mother chose this route? After all, Marisol was Indian. Perhaps this was what she was sent to learn, Morgana reasoned. Still, the Indian burial was alien to her. Her heart broke, remembering the gentle white mare that Isadora so treasured and the way Eagle Eyes had shot her, as if it had died when Isadora had died. He is a cruel man, she concluded.

She completed her sixth log and still he was not back. The quiet stillness of the mountain and the glorious power of the fragrant cedars were making her drowsy in a hypnotic way. She sat cross-legged with the log braced on her knee. Her dress, stained with green from the weeds and grass, felt hot against her skin. She longed for a drink, but he had not left the water pouch and as the hours passed, she found herself extremely hungry. The hunger she could brush from her mind, but her thirst had not ceased and grew like a quest unfulfilled.

Morgana pulled the next log upon her lap, not caring if it tore her dress, and began hacking at the log. Her hands bled freely, making the knife's handle slippery.

"Why isn't this all prepared in advance?" she complained loudly expecting to hear an answer from the stillness that encircled her. Still, she heard nothing but a bird's call and the gentle wind against her perspiring face.

She was totally exhausted upon completing the eighth log. Within an hour, it would be dark and cold. Still, he had not returned. She didn't care, she reasoned, as she lay back against the sharp cedar pines, tucking her abused hands under her armpits for warmth. Soon she fell into a deep sleep.

Suddenly, he was on his knees before her. "Wake!" Eagle Eyes commanded. "You fell asleep. It is dark, we must return to camp."

He helped steady her as she got to her feet, then he bent to pick up the knife she'd used and the other remaining logs. He moved before her in a manner indicating that she should follow him. He walked slowly and glanced back several times to check upon her pace. She weaved from side to side as she walked as if drained of all energy. Suddenly, she collapsed.

He put the logs down, gathered her in his arms. He took the unconscious Morgana to a small running brook that bubbled over small rocks and larger boulders, then rushed downhill as if it were a quickly moving snake, gleaming reflectively in the twilight hour. Near the edge of the brook, he found a clearing where he gently placed her. Then he examined her bloody hands and felt the fever that encircled her head like a crown of thorns.

He shook his head; the fever he had not expected. Her entire body was hot to touch. He picked her up and moved cautiously into the cold water that rushed between his sturdy legs. He knew it was the season for Rocky Mountain fever and hoped her fever was just a case of a disturbed soul, with which he could easily deal. When the water reached higher than his knees, he knelt and slowly allowed her to submerge, feet first.

The bubbling water, cold as if rinsed with freshly fallen snow, caused her to awake screaming. She gasped as he quickly submerged her—head and all. She struggled as he held her down to make sure she was entirely saturated—then he quickly let her up. The intense shock of the cold water made her fall unconscious.

Chapter 5

Eagle Eyes lifted Morgana, then quickly carried her to the sweat lodge on the sacred mountain which was to be their shelter for the next three days. He placed her on a blanket, then went to his warrior horse for a thick bear skin with which to cover her.

He chanted softly as he worked seeking the source of her sudden illness—the unsightly tick that spread the Rocky Mountain fever which allowed its poison to seep into her blood system. He found the tick on the back of her left calf. The area around it appeared red and slightly swollen. He placed the brightly burning tip of a branch upon the tick, causing it to fall off her skin. Then he flung the tick into the fire.

The warm bear skin was slowly layered over her body, starting at her feet. He placed his hand over her forehead and found her temperature had eased. Still, her face remained flushed and clammy, and he knew she was in for a very rough time. He heard the wind howl outside the small lodge, then sat still a moment and listened.

Yes, he thought, I hear you calling, Isadora, for you are as powerful in death as in life. He hurried out of the sweat lodge and whistled to his warrior horse as he walked over to the travois that held Isadora. Falling upon one knee, he studied Isadora's face and found it peaceful. He recognized the glow as one possessed only by those who have lived their lives in accordance with universal laws. He smiled, thinking how much more clever she was than he. Even in death, she pressured him to achieve, to complete tasks, to move forward and to overcome all.

Now, in this situation, he must do his best or else he would lose this troublesome young woman, known among the tribe as Isadora's half-breed treasure.

"Isadora," he declared, "what a web you have woven! Have you decided on the outcome?" he laughed, a deep throaty laugh. "I see we shall be at wit's end against one another, but this time you sleep soundly in death. Yes, you are master, but you have raised me as your successor and I have my feet firmly planted in both worlds. I want to be chief, as great as Geronimo and Red Eagle. My war shall not be of guns and battles, but against social injustice, poverty, prejudice and political greed. I see no place in my life with this woman."

"You, Isadora, saw to my education. You sent me to the white man's university and supported me until I graduated. I learned a great deal and I owe you much; but, this woman is still a half breed and bears a price tag that I refuse to pay even if it is a reciprocation for your favors." He rose, hitched the travois to his horse and slowly led him out of camp toward Isadora's final resting place.

Within the hour, a shrill yell, strong enough to shatter the most delicate crystal, pierced the mountain's atmosphere. His final farewell to Isadora would leave him speechless for many hours.

♡　♡　♡

Another day passed. Eagle Eyes sat with Morgana while she tossed, muttered, cried and screamed countless times. Her hazel eyes opened wildly; yet, they saw nothing, reflecting only sheer terror. At times, they darkened to an almost primitive gray, seeing only the outskirts of a world far away from his quiet chant.

He forced a brewed tea made of yellow dock down her throat, but she merely gazed at him, then proceeded to throw up. He patiently cleaned her face and blanket, then once again made her take the strong muddy drink, hoping that some of it would reach her stomach where it would fight the poisons within her.

It was well into the early morning hours. He was exhausted. He wanted to sleep so he took a safety precaution and tied both her wrists together, then tied the other end of the rope to his arm so that he would sense any movement she might make. Now she slept, but he knew very well there existed the possibility of her sleep walking, crazy with fever as she was, and the strap would prevent her from roaming away. He knew she could become much like a rabid dog before this dreadful illness passed, and he must protect her as well as himself.

He lay down a little away from her and glanced at her profile. Her face seemed carved of wax, a seemingly transparent mask that reflected a strong light of inner beauty. Her nose was not flat against her face, but rather pointed. Her eyelashes were long and almost blue-black in essence.

Indian girls were taught to please others. What, he wondered, had this half-breed been taught? With an Indian mother, she should be knowledgeable in all domestic areas. A Mexican father, he'd heard, did not like sharing his wife or daughters, and kept them tightly in reins by having them securely settled in the home. Still, Morgana seemed to have been raised differently. She seemed the type who gets what she wants, a bit overly concerned with her own little world and the things Isadora had taught her. With his mind filled with such thoughts he fell into a troubled sleep.

In the coolness of dawn, an owl screeched. He awoke instantly. He glanced at Morgana and reached out to touch her forehead. Her fever had risen. Once again, he took her to the brook, but this time she did not even become conscious.

Eagle Eyes knew of the eruptions that would soon blister her skin if the progress of the disease was not altered. He had witnessed several cases with Gold Rod, the neighboring medicine man. As the hours rolled by, his chance of getting the fever down decreased and he worried.

She was resting peacefully after the last icy cold submersion in the creek. He sat opposite her, waiting for the fever to pass, thinking of all the possible remedies he might have overlooked. The herbal paste made of jimson weed he continued to rub on her hands. He forced into her mouth the strong tea made of quinona bark or "cinchona" to prevent her stomach from cramping. The fever rose, then subsided; yet, he kept the medicine drink near her side. The yellow dock brew helped to thin her blood. The dryness of her mouth and the thick brown film that now coated the inside of her mouth were relieved by the same brew.

With all his knowledge he felt helpless. The only other alternative was to take her to a doctor in Santa Fe, but by doing this, he would be breaking the ritual rules of the burial—that he stay four days in mourning. He worried because if he should wait any longer, she might not make it. She was growing weaker by the hour, and now as he quietly chanted, he feared that, perhaps, it was already too late. The drive into Santa Fe would take at least three hours, but his indecision increased as did his fears.

He knelt near her and touched her forehead—nothing had changed. He closed his eyes and prayed to Mother Earth to spare her so that she might continue her trade for the benefit of others. With smoke made from sweetgrass, he purified the fevered young woman; still his worry increased.

Into the middle of the third day, he realized that he had not eaten. As his hunger increased, his desire for food decreased, and he felt his body respond with inner tremors. If he decided to leave the mountain and take her to Santa Fe, he would not be able to muster the strength the trip would require.

He rose and went to his stallion and pulled a piece of dried meat from the bag. He'd boiled the water the previous night so he knew it to be safe. The stallion nuzzled him, then turned his attention back to the wild grass around the area. Eagle Eyes spoke gently to his stallion saying, "You will lead us back to the reservation. Yes, eat and be strong for I will need you more than ever to help me overcome this situation." The stallion snorted gently as if saying he fully understood him.

Eagle Eyes chewed on a piece of the dried meat and then returned to the sweat lodge. He stopped short when he saw brown foam bubbling from

Morgana's mouth. The end is near, he thought to himself sadly. He knelt next to her, gently placing her head on his knee; then, he took a piece of cloth and carefully wiped her mouth. She was unconscious and he knew her spirit was traveling to the crossing point.

"Her death would be such a waste," he moaned. "Forgive me, Great Spirit, forgive me Isadora, but I must take her to the hospital. Great Spirit, shame me not for relenting, but she is only half-clan and belongs to both worlds. I must take her back." He rose quietly and prepared the stallion. On the travois that once held Isadora, he placed Morgana and tied her securely in place. He gave the stallion its head, anxiously urging him to return to the reservation as quickly as possible.

In his own mind, he knew he would have some explaining to do to the outside authorities if she died. The Indians, on the other hand, would think that it had been her fate to die and they would go about their activities not bothering to question him further.

The ride was as long as it was rough. He glanced back to reassure himself that she did not physically sense any pain and he urged the stallion to go faster.

In front of his hut on the reservation, he dismounted and called to his woman servant to tend to Morgana and to a boy to tend to his horse. He quickly changed and prepared blankets and pillows in his jeep, then carried her to the jeep and settled her in the back seat. He was about to drive off toward town when Bittersweet flagged him down. "Her mother," she said, pointing to Morgana, "waits at the first hut."

He cursed as he drove the jeep quickly in the direction of the hut, slamming on the brakes when he saw Marisol. He noted that mother and daughter were almost mirror images except that the younger one was of a fairer complexion. "Hurry!" he demanded, as he pushed open the door and pulled her inside the jeep. "We need to get to the hospital in Santa Fe."

Alarmed, Marisol quickly turned and studied Morgana, who lay prone in the back seat. "What has happened?"

"Rocky Mountain fever," he said firmly.

Marisol gasped sharply, then cried, "No! Not my daughter!" She then managed to cross over to the back seat to be near Morgana.

Eagle Eyes drove as fast as he could, concentrating on the highway to Santa Fe. From the rear view mirror he watched as Marisol gently took Morgana in her arms and spoke in a hushed whispering voice to her. He heard Morgana say, "Mother."

"Shh!" Marisol answered. "You are in good hands and all will be well soon. Rest now."

Eagle Eyes wondered whose hands Marisol was referring to. Perhaps the Great Spirit, he thought, or maybe her own hands. Mothers had a knack for calming down restless off-spring ... but then, how would he know for sure? The only mother he had known had been his old aunt. She had tried to make up for the loss of his mother who had passed on when he was only three. As luck would have it, she too passed on. Then came Isadora who comforted him, pushed him, encouraged him—and now she too was gone.

He shook his head slowly, acknowledging to himself how hard his luck had been during those most impressionable years. Yes, Isadora had been there. His father, Bold Feather, had immersed himself into tribal politics and had been too busy to notice the needs of the small boy. How he had needed his love—but, as destined, Bold Feather also passed when Eagle Eyes was ten, and then he belonged totally to Isadora.

It had been Isadora who found him near death after a week of raging fever, alone, in his father's house, without food or care. It had been Isadora who tended and cured him, and it had been because of her that he had eventually regained his strength, his spirit and his ambition.

Remember, he reminisced, the law of nature is that if something is taken away, something else must be given back to compensate. Gone were his mother, his father, his aunt; and in turn, he received from each of them many acres of reservation land, houses, huts and a hefty monthly stipend from the government.

But from Isadora, he learned not to need money, to live simply, to give to others in whatever way he could, to love the land and one's freedom. It was in his father's house on the reservation that he still lived while doing business there. His father's old friends tended his cattle, his horses and his lands while he learned about the medicines, the chants, the cures at the same time he received his law degree. Without these persons around him, he would be nothing! His sincere appreciation went very deep and if they ever had a need, he would do his utmost to help them.

He glanced back and saw that Marisol held Morgana in a tight embrace. Sensing the man's eyes upon her, Marisol studied his face a moment before asking in a whisper, "Did you touch her?"

He was stunned to the point of outrage because Indian women did not ask Indian men such questions. He hesitated before answering, "She is as she came!"

To his surprise the woman started weeping.

"Why do you weep? Surely, she is no virgin!" he snapped.

"She is such," replied the mother. "Her virginity is of great value to her father."

He spoke no more, but kept his eyes on the road and drove the remaining distance in silence.

"My daughter burns hotter than the fires of the underworld!" declared the anxious mother.

"We have arrived." Eagle Eyes maneuvered the jeep into the emergency parking area of the small hospital and called out to the two nurses who stood near the door. He took Morgana into his arms and placed her on the stretcher, explaining the symptoms to the nurses as they entered the foyer, then went into a small examining room. They quickly drew the curtains, leaving the tired Indian waiting helplessly outside and Marisol wringing her hands.

Finally Marisol gently touched his arm, unsure as she was of his response. "Come, we can sit over here."

He followed reluctantly, removed his hat and nervously tapped it against the side of his leg, never removing his eyes from the tightly drawn curtain that sealed the examining room.

Marisol rose. "I must call my husband," she said.

Stunned, he rose quickly, merely nodded, and let her pass. So, he thought, I will meet him, too. He nervously started pacing the floor. How would this man react to all that had happened to his daughter? He decided that he would handle her father with diplomacy and honesty. After all, what else could he possibly do?

As Marisol walked toward him, Eagle Eyes noticed that her eyes remained downcast and she kept her hands clasped in front of her, as if letting them lead her wherever she wanted to go. She looked delicate and submissive, as if all the fight had evaporated from her body and she had simply accepted her fate. Still, even at her age, he could see her beauty.

"My husband is on his way." She crossed in front of him, then turned and said, "He is not Indian. He is Mexican and his feelings will be exploding in anger, as is his way, but please be patient as was your father."

"You knew my father?" he asked. So surprised was he that his hat dropped to the floor.

"Yes, Rusty," she replied, "many years ago." A sad look flickered across her face, then she flushed when she realized she had his full attention.

"Continue, please ... how old were you?"

"We were young, you see—we grew up together and we—we liked each other very much."

"Did you know my mother also?" he asked, looking away from her face to hide his anxiety.

"No, she was from another area—her family came from high in the mountains. I saw her at her marriage feast. She looked happy, but she was so much younger than your father." She rubbed her hands nervously and remained silent for a long while before continuing. "I dreamed of our ...

well, you look so much like him—so strong, so young and so challenging. There is much sadness in your eyes."

"As in yours," he responded.

She rose and paced the floor. "Yes," she muttered.

"Go on, tell me what happened. You are leaving out something, aren't you?"

She pivoted and glanced at him skeptically, but did not speak.

"Your reluctance to speak of him leads me to believe that you and my father were more than acquaintances or even friends."

As was her way, Marisol studied her hands. "It was so long ago and my memories are my own."

"That answer is neither a yes or a no!" he retaliated.

"Is life ever as simple as a yes or no?" she replied quietly.

"Mrs. Cruz," the nurse spoke, "the doctor will see you now. Please follow me."

They both hurriedly followed her down the long corridor. Eagle Eyes studied the worried woman beside him, then said, "You know my first name. How is that?"

Marisol hesitated a moment and said, "We can talk later, if you must."

"Indeed I must!" answered Eagle Eyes. They entered a small hospital room.

Marisol rushed to the bed where Morgana lay looking gravely ill. Her skin was the color of a dirty gray glove with embedded red splotches and her hands were heavily bandaged. A bag of glucose and another of a different medication hung from each side of the bed.

The doctor, standing next to Morgana, had just finished his examination and motioned to Eagle Eyes to follow him out to the hall to talk. Marisol followed both men out to the hallway. "I'm Dr. Ramirez." He shook hands with Eagle Eyes. "Your wife is ... "

"She is not my wife." Eagle Eyes quietly corrected the doctor.

"She is my daughter," Marisol said as she stepped closer to the doctor. "Tell me everything, please."

A surprised look flashed across the doctor's face. Indian women were not so outrightly bold as this woman. He turned to Eagle Eyes for confirmation.

Eagle Eyes simply nodded and stood with his hand in his jean pockets as the doctor began. "Well, she's very ill, but I think you've gotten her here in time. I have her on antibiotics—tetracycline, to be exact. It'll be three or four days before her fever comes down. Until that time, we just have to wait and watch her closely. Her hands are healing. The salve on them was hard to wash off, but it worked excellently." He looked at Marisol. "Mind telling me what it was?"

A puzzled look crossed Marisol's face as she turned to Eagle Eyes. "I don't know. He took care of her."

The doctor crossed his arms as if in deep thought. "Interesting," he added. "I'm doing some research on herbal medicine. Would you like to talk sometime?"

"I would like to know about her!" Eagle Eyes snapped angrily.

"Right! She is still unconscious, but she shouldn't have any problems once the medicine starts to work. It was a close call, but it seems she was well taken care of during this ordeal. Her mouth will be very sore, so there will be some weight loss. I suggest her mother stay here with her for the first day at least."

Marisol nodded her agreement as the doctor continued. "There are papers to sign. If you'll come this way," Dr. Ramirez added, as he took Marisol's elbow and walked down the corridor to a small office.

Eagle Eyes turned and watched them disappear into the office before he entered the small room. He stood at the door a moment as if summoning up the courage to go to Morgana. He had failed her by succumbing to his own fears. Why had his faith in his own medicine vanished? With Morgana he felt a deep inability to treat her medically as he had done for countless other members of his tribe.

Morgana frightened him, perhaps, he thought to himself, because she seemed so flawless, because she also was taught by Isadora, and because she had each foot planted in a different worlds as he did. Her world of Mexican and Indian cultures, he was sure, created conflict as his mix of Anglo and Indian traditions challenged him at times.

In law school he was whispered about because he wore his hair long and braided. Because of his vest, jeans and well-worn boots. He used his strange personality and his unusual dress as his chief defense against all those law students whose socks matched and whose expensive loafers were spit-shined daily. But, now, that episode of his past was something he laughed about over a cold beer.

Those unnecessary rituals of youth, he mused! In large cities, he found appearances were more valued than grades. God, if only he could do all those years over, if only he could have cared more, if only he could change all that needed to be changed. Then he wouldn't be such a hard-nosed Indian who appeared untouchable.

He laughed to himself, shaking his head as he approached Morgana's hospital bed and studied her. She, who seemed so defenseless now, caused his locked-up memories to flood forward to haunt him. He gently touched her forehead and realized that the fever was at last receding.

"It is just about over, my pretty flower," he said. "You will do fine." He bent over and kissed her forehead, lingering there a moment. Then he kissed her cheek as he whispered encouragingly in her ear.

Suddenly, he realized that someone was standing in the dark recesses of the door. He straightened himself up, then turned to see a silver-haired man approach the bed.

The man glanced boldly at Eagle Eyes with eyes as emerald as the sea and then stood on the opposite side of the bed, sizing up the strong young man before him. After a long, tense moment, he took his daughter's hand and placed a long loving kiss and caress upon it—all the while gazing down sadly at her.

Eagle Eyes realized that this man dressed in jeans, boots, and a pearl button plaid western shirt was none other than Morgana's father. He stepped away and moved toward the door.

"Wait up here!" The voice was not angry—it was definitely forceful but not angry. Eagle Eyes turned toward the man and listened. "I understand you've been with my daughter these last three days. Is that right?" His green eyes blazed steadily at the Indian, letting him know that he was in charge.

"Yes, her presence was requested at Isadora's burial."

"My daughter answers to no one but me! I shall charge you with kidnapping!" he growled furiously. "Now look at her condition! *¡Qué lástima!* What a pity!"

Legally he was right, thought Eagle Eyes. She had not consented to go, but he decided to remain unresponsive and cool, allowing the man to blow off steam. So he merely stared back at the old man and waited.

"My wife and I were worried sick about her. If she does not pull through, I'm going to hold you personally responsible and that means—I'm going to cut your throat!"

"Don't you understand that Isadora is dead and ... "

"Isadora has been nothing but a thorn in my side since the day I married my wife. I thought I'd broken Isadora's control over my women ... but no! No! Isadora is forever there! Isadora! *¡Esa bruja no vale!* That witch is no good!"

"Stop!" commanded Eagle Eyes as he approached the Mexican. "You know nothing of the situation!" He pointed to Morgana. "Wait until she can speak and explain her actions, for she is, as you fail to see, a grown woman!"

"*¡Vete, hombre!* Go, man!"

"Ohhhh," Morgana moaned helplessly in her sleep. Both men stopped arguing and rushed to her side. Again she slipped back into unconsciousness.

Eagle Eyes watched her a moment, glanced up at the man and stormed out of the room. "What is done, is done!"

Chapter 6

Morgana felt her head spinning round and round. She could hear her father's voice and wondered what she could have done to make him so angry. Knots tore up her insides. Now Eagle Eye's voice penetrated her senses. He too was angry. Oh, how dry her mouth was and how she wished she could swim in the cold spring to douse the heat that consumed her body. How she longed for the smell of the clean, powerful cedar trees that filled the mountain tops. When would her head stop spinning? She wanted to grab hold of something sturdy to stop the spinning. Only blackness surrounded her as the voices receded.

After a while the spinning stopped to almost a slight motion as if she were riding upon gentle rolling waves. The waves stopped and before her glowed a bright light. Through the light Isadora stood regally before her, cautiously telling Morgana to go back.

"No, my daughter, it is not time for you. You have much work to do for the Great Spirit." Isadora raised her arm and waved Morgana away. "Go back! Farewell, my daughter!"

Morgana protested, "Isadora! Don't leave me!" she screamed as Isadora's image slowly faded in the cool, thin mist that encircled her, and she could no longer see anything but heavy darkness. Soon she slept.

When she awoke, she found herself screaming for her mother. A chill seeped through the sheet and blanket that covered her in the hospital room. Her eyes darted quickly around the room, seeking a comforting presence. Finding herself alone, she settled back into the groove her head had made in the pillow and began collecting her thoughts. She glanced up at the intravenous bag that dangled at her bedside. Raising her hands, she gasped at the sight of the bruises and cuts that caused them to be stiff and swollen.

Sadness overcame her as she remembered the battle she had endured while cleaning the trees and how the hardness in the Indian's eyes had not softened as she worked frantically to prove that she was fit to get the job done. Had she completed the task, she wondered? Then she remembered that a sense of fatigue had overtaken her so suddenly that she had been forced to lay back.

The arrogant Indian had smirked in his pleasure at finding her nearly unconscious and, regardless of her condition, he had commanded her to follow him. Wasn't that exactly how Indian men treated their women—as if they were stepping stones?

What time was it now? She tried to sit up, only to find that her head seemed to be carrying an extra ten pounds of weight. Dizziness overtook her and she closed her eyes again.

When Marisol returned from the hospital cafeteria, she peered down anxiously at her daughter, who had obviously moved because the sheet and blanket were disarranged, leaving her arms and hands exposed. She must have regained consciousness, Marisol concluded. Perhaps she'd awake again soon.

Marisol wanted to be there to reassure Morgana that everything was all right: that Isadora's body finally rested, that Eagle Eyes was the son of her old lover, Bold Feather, that she was completely taken by him, and that Frank Cruz had made a generous donation to the Church in Santa Fe hoping to intercede with the Catholic saints on his daughter's behalf (something he'd never done before in his entire life). Since he was not a religious man, it was out of character for him to do such a thing; still it pleased Marisol that her husband was humble enough to fall on his knees in church and plead with God for help.

"Morganita," she softly whispered in her ear, "I think you have met your future husband; he is all that I desire for you. He has property and knowledge and he is handsome. The match would please me greatly." She hesitated a moment before adding, "He seems so right for you. Oh, I am eternally grateful for Isadora for this arrangement."

At the same time that Marisol sat quietly with her thoughts, Frank Cruz paced the hospital floor like a caged tiger. "Why won't she wake?" cried Cruz. "It's been two days! Stupid Indian, exposing my girl like he did. I should cut his throat!"

His anger and annoyance blinded him so that he failed to see his wife flinch, then shrink back as if the corner would protect her from his verbal declaration of war. He fled the room and she knew he would seek out and find the doctor, needling him for an explanation in both Spanish and English as to why his daughter had not awakened.

A tray crashed to the floor in the hallway. Morgana woke up screaming and bolted up in bed. "Mother!" she cried.

Marisol hurried to the bedside. "Take care, my daughter," she whispered, as she cradled her daughter in her arms.

"Mother, I have felt so horrible . . . so awful!"

Marisol felt her daughter tremble. "It's over," she said, "and you are safe. Eagle Eyes meant no harm. Your father and I are here."

"Eagle Eyes was so . . . insensitive! He's a mean person, Mother!"

Marisol shook her head. "The circumstances of your meeting have caused all this confusion. Eagle Eyes is very worried about you. If only you could have seen him, as I saw him, waiting in the emergency room, pacing just as your father is doing now. He ... "

The door swung open and Frank Cruz rushed in. *"Hija*, how do you feel? I think you should rest more, for you don't look well!"

"Father!" she muttered. "I'm so glad you're here."

He embraced her. "I was so worried, but the doctors assured me that you'd be fine and for that I will give the biggest fiesta Santa Fe and Taos have ever seen!" He kissed the top of her head.

"Father, I'm not ready for a fiesta," she added, realizing that he would pay no attention to her. She stroked his arm, drawing strength from it.

He laughed. "Of course you're not ready yet, but when you recover, daughter. In the meantime, your mother can start the invitation list. I want everyone to attend. I'll slaughter several goats for barbecue. Then I'll have a large tent set up and bring in some Indian women to do the kitchen work. The Mariachi Los Rayos de Santa Fe can supply the entertainment and we can gear up the stallion and La Luna for a riding exhibition."

Morgana slowly eased herself down upon the pillow, too exhausted to speak. All his plans made her head spin again. *"Por Dios*, for God's sake, Papa, please. I feel so tired."

"Old man! You tire her! Let her rest!" Marisol commanded.

"¡Sí! Yes, yes!" he continued. "But let's make a list of guests for the fiesta while she rests."

"¡Hombre loco! Crazy man!" muttered Marisol as she fussed over Morgana's covers.

♡   ♡   ♡

Three weeks later Morgana stood on her balcony, half hidden in the shadows, surveying the fiesta below. True to his word, her Papa had managed to draw a large crowd of friends from Santa Fe and Taos to celebrate her getting well. The people below, many of whom she'd known for years, were feasting on *fajitas, cabrito*, salads, Indian corn cakes and other treats. Some were smiling, some dancing to a *conjunto* band and most were crowding around the portable bar that had been set up.

Morgana knew that it was going to be a party in which people would stay late. Her father and his buddies would be singing *"Las Mañanitas"* somewhere between the hours of three and four in the morning—drunk, laughing until their laughter echoed through the mountains.

When she was in her early teens, these fiestas were all she could think about for days before and days after the party. Her senses were high strung, like a newly tuned guitar, and her laughter could be heard by everyone, for she was happy, young and naive. Now, as she gazed down below, she did not feel happy, nor did she feel like going downstairs to join the merry makers. Instead, she felt like running away.

Just run, she thought, and keep running, just as she had done for her "*Kinaalda*," her "Indian coming of age" ceremony. Marisol and Isadora had arranged the special ceremony without her father's knowing. Morgana smiled to herself. To this day, her father did not know about the celebration which had been held in Isadora's hogan.

According to the Navajo custom, it had been time for Morgana to leave her childhood behind and to become a woman. She had to run as long and as hard as she could while being chased by a large group of children whose age matched hers and whose objective was to capture her. If she outran them, then she would live a long, healthy life. She remembered how Isadora washed her long hair in yucca suds before she was dressed in the long skirt and long-sleeved blouse of the traditional Navajo woman's costume. Then Isadora smeared her face with white paint. She remembered how the group of strange older women frightened her as they chanted, then danced. She had continuously glanced at her mother seeking encouragement, for she had been very frightened. Who were those strange children who would be chasing her, intending to cut her down like a stricken rabbit if given the opportunity? She had not known them. The whole ceremony had been strange to her, but Marisol and Isadora insisted that she go through it.

Marisol had explained to Morgana that while she was out "racing" with the children, the older women had sung chants and also had said prayers for her well-being. These prayers had been the same that the original holy people had chanted at the beginning of time.

The older women had also baked a great ceremonial cake for her and the other guests. They had poured buckets of batter, much like corn cakes, into an outdoor oven. Then, they had cautiously covered the cake with corn shucks, forming crosses over the batter as they had sang, "She is preparing for her child. The spirit of our supreme mother, Changing Woman, prepares to acknowledge her new daughter, Morgana."

The children had not caught Morgana. She had raced into the hogan with her heart beating as if it would burst. Her lungs ached so that she felt as if she would never breathe normally again. She had flung herself at Isadora, who held her tightly in her arms, gently stroking her hair until her heart stopped racing and her lungs stopped burning. It had been Isadora who had kissed her on her forehead repeatedly while Marisol had looked on with tears streaming from her eyes. How angry her father would have been if he'd found out about the secret ceremony and about how she had drawn strength from it, often relying on the Indian women for support.

For Morgana, her *"Kinaalda"* had been a very painful ceremony and had contrasted sharply with her *"Quinceañera"* or her "Fifteenth Birthday" celebration.

Her parents had planned for the *"Quinceañera"* a year in advance. They had formally visited each family that was to serve as a sponsor, as well as the families of the fourteen young girls that were to be members of her court of honor called *"damas"*. How exciting it was for each girl to ask a young man to escort her to the celebration. The formal dresses of pink silk organza were ordered months in advance. It had been so difficult for Morgana to pick her dress, for she had liked several. With time running out, she settled on a pink lace dress beaded with small delicate pearls and matching elbow length gloves. The hotel in Santa Fe had been reserved months in advance and her father had gladly paid their huge fee, while Marisol gasped in disapproval.

The mass at the cathedral had been scheduled for three in the afternoon followed by the dinner. It had been during mass that she had pledged her love to God and her parents. Seeing her father's green eyes brimming with tears, she had almost lost her composure. Her father had never cried before; yet, he had wiped his eyes like a woman in mourning. She had not understood it. Marisol had been stunned by the glitter and grandness of the occasion; yet, Morgana had thought her mother had looked beautiful in her blue silk dress and silver shoes.

After dinner the grand dance had started with the formal presentation of her parents and her court. It had been a magical time, a day Morgana had wished would never end. For her father the *"Quinceañera"* had been the first step toward a formal wedding ceremony and for his only daughter he had not minded the expense. Marisol, on the other hand, had sincerely wanted the day to pass quickly so they could return home to her treasured simpler life.

♡   ♡   ♡

Morgana leaned over the stone ledge of the balcony. She searched the milling crowd for Marisol, who she knew would be dressed in her black leather Indian dress and soft doe skin boots. Inwardly she smiled, for her mother had her own way of rebelling against her father. By refusing to dress in the traditional Mexican costume, Marisol had learned to stand her ground against his wishes. "I am not Mexican," she would say. It was the only time she displayed any type of defiance toward him. Morgana glanced to the back towards the pavilion where the Mexicans were gathered and did not see her.

She knew her mother's Indian friends could be found in the kitchen or in the back section of the house. The Indians talked in whispered tones, clinging to each other in order not to socialize with the other invited guests. It was always thus and Morgana had learned early to remove herself from one group to visit with the other until she eventually found herself in the kitchen speaking with her mother's Indian friends. Knowing that she was a part of both groups, she made a conscious effort to make everyone feel at home even though she never fully understood the reasoning behind the noticeable groupings by race.

Marisol would wish everyone welcome, greeting them in the proper tones. But, as soon as she suspected that all the guests were present, she would conveniently disappear into the kitchen to supervise the various dishes before she made her midnight escape to her bedroom for the remainder of the night. It was at this time that Morgana would play hostess until two in the morning. By then, everyone would have gone home except Papa's closest drinking buddies. Then, she too, would have retreated to her room to shower and to call it a night.

As Morgana stood on the balcony, she remembered the day when Isadora had decided to attend one of her father's fiestas. Isadora's entrance had been ignored by most of the guests, except the Indians who had quickly gathered around her and drawn her to a special spot. Morgana had been about ten years old. She had eagerly taken Isadora's hand and led her to Marisol, who had bowed to the old woman to show her respect. Yet, it had not been until Isadora had reached out and heartily embraced Marisol that Morgana had sensed their unusual bonding. Isadora had had the ability to make her mother smile happily once again. Morgana had then decided not to leave Isadora's side until the party ended.

Her father had been very angry when he had found her in her fine party dress sitting on a blanket that had been placed upon the dirt, graciously holding Isadora's plate of food. Try as he might, he had not been able to pry his daughter away from the straight-backed Indian woman.

Upstairs in her room, Morgana now glanced up toward the giant mountain which secured the back side of the house. It was still twilight and the glow from the party lamps cast shadows that made the boulders seem larger and more ominous. She noted a movement, perhaps a coyote, but ignored it and glanced up at the sky, a hazy gray in color, streaked with pinks and oranges.

Morgana moved back inside and looked at herself in the mirror. For this party she had dressed in her turquoise-colored full-skirt adorned with the silver concho belt. She had on her Spanish boots and velvet Indian vest that Marisol had handmade for her. She was aware that her outfit represented the various cultures that were embedded in her soul. Still, she lacked the exuberance that had been evident in her personality before the illness of the last four weeks, and something else was missing, something she still could not identify. She felt like climbing to the top of the mountain to get away from the party below.

Just then Marisol rapped gently on the door. "Morgana, daughter," she said.

"Coming, Mother!" Morgana pivoted in time to encounter her mother as she entered the room.

"You look so nice." Marisol went to the balcony to peek below, then added, "Your father is having a good time, as usual."

"Mother, I just don't feel like partying."

Marisol quickly touched her forehead. "You're not ill, are you?"

"I feel strange, as if part of me is still sleeping like Isadora. I feel like a net has encircled my heart. At first I thought it was the medicine I've been taking and hoped it would disappear with time, but it has not."

"You have been through a lot, daughter, and we shall talk later. For now, there are gifts for you to open and guests to thank. The more quickly it is done the better. Then you can rest. Come."

"Okay, give me a moment and then I'll be down."

"Do not take too long!" As Marisol moved to the door, she was unable to conceal the worried look that covered her face.

Morgana noticed that the moon now peeked through the star-studded sky. She took several deep breaths, then turned reluctantly to go downstairs. She walked slowly down the stairs to the foyer of the house. There, she hesitated, and forced herself to smile. Then she slowly opened the door and went outside to the patio.

Mr. and Mrs. Ramos, owners of a book store in Taos, approached her. "You look well. No one would know you've been ill," Mrs. Ramos commented as she handed Morgana a small gift-wrapped box. Mr. Ramos kissed her palm and smiled, then quickly turned his attention to where the men were grouped, not even hearing Morgana's whispered "Thank you."

The Mariachi started playing, encircling Morgana to serenade her. Oh, Father, she thought sadly, for she knew he so wanted her to be happy, but she did not feel happy. She stood and listened to their song of greetings, sensing everyone's eyes upon her, then smiled because it was expected of her.

Her father joined her. Laughing and clapping his hands vigorously, encouraging the crowd to pick up the fast beat, he gently took his daughter by her elbow and led her to the center of the patio, where he bowed slightly to her. She curtsied, slightly holding the ends of her full skirt high in her arms, allowing the turquoise hue to flow around her. His eyes told no tales, for he was extremely proud of his daughter as he led her through the intricate steps of the Mexican Polka. How proudly she held her head, how enchantingly she smiled.

Yes, he smiled through his thin moustache. She was always one to make him proud. Never mind he'd never had sons, she was all he adored, all he loved. Yes, he could love Marisol more, but she would never let him get close to her heart as his daughter did. Marisol's nature was reserved, he reasoned, knowing full well that his wife and his daughter would be the only women in his life. All that he had was theirs. He smiled mischievously. What would their reaction be if they knew of the tunnel full of silver ore that he'd discovered ages ago? He would never let them know about the silver tunnel until he felt the time was just right for them to know his secret.

The dance ended and the guests applauded. Morgana bowed demurely, smiling all the while, yet searching the crowd for Marisol.

"Now, she will cut her cake. Please follow us, my friends." Her father led her over to the center of the table where a many-tiered cake iced in chocolate waited. She took a long silver cake knife and sliced a piece for her father, then smiled to see Marisol join them at the table. The second piece she handed to her mother. Finally, she sliced her own and stood for photographs with the two most important people in her world. And as the flash bulbs flared, Morgana saw at the back of the crowd a man with an eye patch. In a flash of a second the man had disappeared. Morgana looked the crowd over, then asked, "Mother, can we wait for a while before I open the gifts?"

"Yes, it is as you wish, but do you not feel well?"

"I'll be fine. I'll step over there and get a cold drink. That should help."

She moved quickly towards the portable bar, smiling and greeting people as she hurried past them. Upon reaching the bar, she reached out for a cold drink. This should calm my nerves, she thought, as she turned to survey the guests who were clustered in small groups laughing and talking.

The man with the eye patch had disappeared and was nowhere to be seen. She felt herself shiver slightly—her spirit more dampened than ever as her mind searched her memory for a clue as to who he might be. She gulped her drink, her eyes darting from person to person, seeking the olive skinned man with black wavy hair and the black eye patch, but she did not find him.

Suddenly she heard a voice calling out her name.

"Isadora?" she whispered, hurrying to the kitchen entrance. "Have you seen Mother?" she asked an Indian woman, named Corn Flower, who was working in the kitchen.

"No," Corn Flower responded as she turned to study the young woman before her. "You could use more sleep," she added in a concerned voice. Morgana gripped the counter for support.

"Corn Flower, so much has happened since Isadora's passing. I'm so confused and weak—too weak to deal with a lot of what's been happening."

The Indian woman continued to make Indian corn cakes as she nodded knowingly that she understood. "Perhaps you should ask Eagle Eyes for a remedy. You know he can take care of all things."

Morgana glared at the woman, sensing a flurry of emotion spring forward at the mention of Eagle Eyes. Butterflies nervously fluttered in her stomach, creating a nauseating effect. She turned and hurried out of the kitchen through the back door and, once again, found herself among the guests. She moved toward a large boulder which was on higher ground so that she could privately sort out the guests as they danced a country western number. She spotted Marisol near the main table overseeing the food—but she did not see her father nor the strange man with the eye patch. Some small rocks, followed by a vacuum of dust, fell a foot from where she stood. She moved back, glancing up toward the huge boulder directly behind her, when suddenly a hand covered her mouth.

A man forced her back against the shadowed side of the boulder out of sight of anyone. He braced his body against hers so that she could not move. For a long while he stayed there until he was satisfied that the look in her eyes would not betray him to the others. He removed his hand from her lips, then stepped away from her as if to survey her physically.

"Are you well?" he asked.

Morgana chose not to answer. Instead, she studied Eagle Eyes closely, noting his hands were in a tight fist. His black leather vest shimmered in the light from the fiesta, and the silver and turquoise *bolo* kept the collar of his gray silk shirt in place. The dimple on his right cheek creased as his tension mounted. He shifted uncomfortably, then moved toward her and took her hand in his.

"I am concerned. That is why I am here as an uninvited guest."

Still Morgana refused to answer him.

He moved away from the boulder and surveyed the crowded fiesta below, trying to determine if they'd been seen by anyone. Then his gaze fell upon her once again and lingered longer than necessary on her lips. He reached over and pulled her close. Morgana knew better than to fight and allowed him to kiss her. As he kissed her, she found herself breathless.

The band at the party stopped playing and the guests voices loomed louder, putting Eagle Eyes on alert. He immediately withdrew, but hesitated a moment, holding her until she was steady on her feet.

"I shall watch your fiesta from the top of this boulder." He smiled, then disappeared into the dark shadows of the boulder while she leaned against it, wondering how on earth he could climb up the mountain from this side.

Morgana could see Marisol searching for her among the guests. Morgana took a moment to straighten her clothes, then fanned out her long hair, allowing it to fall like silk threads upon her back. She then glanced up to the top of the mountain but she could not see a thing. He is truly like an eagle, she thought, as she moved quietly back into the lights from the many lanterns that blazed around the guests.

"Daughter," Marisol called upon seeing her. "The gifts need to be opened before our guests leave. Come."

She took her daughter's arms, leading her to a special table filled with many gaily wrapped gifts. As was the custom, all the women and girls gathered around to clap and shout their reaction to each gift that was opened. A crystal flower vase, a pair of unusual earrings Morgana knew were privately custom-made, the latest best-seller novel, a pair of gloves, a printed scarf, a gold belt, and a small gold box were some of the gifts. The last gift was wrapped in gleaming silver paper and was stacked on the bottom of all the other gifts. "There's no card," remarked Morgana as she turned the gift to examine it. She quickly tore at the paper and found a black velvet box. The box itself was elaborate, she thought, suddenly feeling frightened.

"Open it!" shouted all the women in unison.

Morgana smiled hesitantly, then glanced at Marisol who had not uttered a word. She slowly pried open the gold-lined lid.

The box contained a necklace the likes of which Morgana had never seen. The inch-wide silver band fell to a sharp V at which point rested a medallion of the finest quality silver. Diamonds formed a cluster at the center of the medallion.

"Gosh almighty!" Morgana gasped, turning to Marisol who immediately jumped to her feet upon seeing such a costly piece of jewelry.

"Surely, there is a card!" Marisol exclaimed as she searched the table and the ground while the other women rushed forward to get a closer look at the necklace.

"It has to be from my father!" Morgana said as she put the box down on the table so that the women could get a better look.

"Most certainly not!" snapped Marisol nervously. "Your father would never spend that kind of money."

"Who then?" Morgana turned to scrutinize the dainty vines embossed on the inch-wide band. She rudely grabbed the velvet box from the excited women and headed toward the house in search of her father. She entered the foyer and then turned toward the den, his favorite spot. Without bothering to knock, she shoved open the doors. "*¡Papá! ¿Dónde estás?* Where are you?" she called.

Frank Cruz stood in front of the fireplace holding a cold beer can. The smile on his face faded when he saw his daughter's frightened eyes. Hurrying to join her he asked, "*¿Qué pasa?* What's happened?"

"Did you give this to me?" she asked, as she opened the box to display the gift.

He stammered, then whistled when he saw the necklace. "I'm afraid not." He shook his head. "Sorry, but it's out of my line and too expensive for my taste," he added softly upon seeing her crushed look.

"There was no card."

A man suddenly rose from the leather chair and cleared his throat to make his presence known to Morgana. When she turned, the stranger involuntarily stepped toward her. "I sent the necklace in hopes of letting your father know how much I appreciate his friendship," he hesitated. "It is a token of our friendship."

"Who are you?" she asked boldly as she moved closer to her father, never once taking her eyes off the black triangular patch that covered the stranger's eye.

"My name is Kelly. I just bought the ranch next door."

"Kelly," interrupted her father, "I think this necklace is much too expensive. Putting friendship aside, I cannot allow my daughter to accept it." He protectively put his arm on his Morgana's shoulders.

Morgana glanced up at the stranger. "The necklace is very beautiful. Any woman would admire it. The women outside were falling all over themselves, but I feel that it's too much since I don't know you." She held the velvet box to him, noting that he hesitated before taking it. "I hope you understand," she added softly, looking away from him.

"I understand," he said, taking the box she held outstretched to him. He glanced at Cruz who was not angry.

¡Qué hombre! What a man, thought Cruz, as he quickly took a gulp of his beer, wondering what this man Kelly was up to. Is he proposing marriage? This man bears watching, he decided, for now I know that he is well off. To merely give her something of great value is sin enough. I will watch him closely.

Mr. Cruz glanced at the blazing fire, remembering the day that he'd first stumbled into Kelly as he'd searched for stray cattle on the land belonging to the neighboring ranch. He had immediately liked the large man with skin as dark as a full-blooded Indian who, in a neighborly fashion, had offered him a cup of steaming coffee and one of the fish he'd just fried. He discovered that Kelly was different and that he was as sharp as a tack. Cruz had enjoyed his company and if Morgana and Kelly became friends, that too would please him. "Please, have a seat, Kelly." Mr. Cruz hastily added, "Daughter, join us, if you will."

Morgana controlled the instinct to flee and chose the seat nearest her father. She sat, solemnly watching the man before her while her father fixed her a glass of chilled wine. Kelly's gleaming and wavy black hair was collar length and his suit was cut to precisely fit his large chest; he was, in fact, she decided, one of the most unusual men she'd met. His skin color distracted her for he looked more Mexican than Indian.

"I hope you're feeling better," Kelly added, his stare taking in her petite size, and the position of her legs. "Your father has told me a lot about you."

Her eyes fell on his ostrich boots, one of which he lifted to rest upon his other leg. His relaxed manner, she noted, did not include his little fingers which were twitching erratically against the fabric of the chair. "Yes, well, I still tire easily."

"She'll be fine!" added Cruz. "She's young, and youth is a powerful asset to have in time of illness. Besides, Morgana is known to do things in a big way. In a few days I'll have her and La Luna riding the high sierras again."

"Father!" she exclaimed, responding to her father's teasing.

Kelly added, "I'd love to ride with you one day, Morgana. Perhaps when you're stronger."

"Yes, when I'm stronger." Feeling uneasy, Morgana rose quickly. "I must return to our guests. Nice meeting you, Mr. Kelly."

Kelly immediately rose and watched her leave the room. "Cruz, I feel like an ass!" he added quickly to the old man who was popping open another can of beer.

"There have been bigger idiots than you, *amigo*," Cruz laughed. "The gift was nice," he added, "but my daughter can't be bought. I know from years of experience. Perhaps I should have introduced you two sooner. Come on, let's get some food." Cruz left the room with Kelly following, then headed for the large tent.

Morgana headed toward the bar. Her thoughts flashed back to the boulder and Eagle Eyes. Involuntarily, she turned toward the boulder, but she could not see a thing because the shadows were too dense. What she needed at this moment was a rescue, a helicopter to zoom her away from all this to a place where there were no pressures, no stress, no doubts. Unfortunately that would happen, she knew, only if one were truly dead.

Chapter 7

It was well after midnight and Morgana knew that Marisol had already retreated to her bedroom. Her father had gathered toward the back with his group of special drinking buddies, and most of the other guests had already left the ranch. Morgana checked the kitchen where the women were cleaning up the remaining pots and pans. They would be leaving within the hour, they said. She then went to the main entrance to see any other guest off. There, under the light of the lamp post, she waited and wondered if Kelly had left as well. She supposed he had, for she had seen him during the party walking from group to group with Papa. She, too, spent her time going from person to person making small talk, assuring everyone that she felt better.

The night air was chilly. Morgana turned toward the house, thinking of nothing but taking off her boots, having a quick shower and then a long undisturbed sleep.

As she stepped up toward the elevated patio, she hesitated, then glanced around to make sure there were no other guests stranded outside. She listened to the laughter of the small cluster of her father's men friends. Then she turned toward the party tent—only the blue flags waved in the now cool increasing wind. Satisfied that all was quiet, she entered the house and closed the door. As she turned, she found herself face to face with Kelly.

"Oh, I thought you'd gone!" she exclaimed with her hand shielding her heart.

He smiled. "Yes, I'm on my way. I just wanted to say good-bye to you." He slowly approached her.

"Thanks for coming, Kelly," she said, then added nervously. "A friend of Father's is a friend of mine ... as they say." She stepped toward the door and politely opened it, then glanced back at him.

He hesitated, then said, "I think that goes, *'Mi casa es su casa'*." He quickly added, "I'd really like to get to know you better."

She turned to the door. "Yes, that would be nice, but I have to recover fully. You understand, don't you?"

"Fine, I'll call you." As he passed her, he turned to look into her eyes.

"Goodnight and thanks for coming," she added quickly, hoping he didn't have thoughts about kissing her.

He nodded, put on his Stetson and left.

She closed the door, then rushed into her room and bolted her door before anyone else could stop her. Now she understood why Marisol disappeared to her room as quickly as possible whenever there was a fiesta. Everyone was caught up in his or her own little scheme of things. Everyone had a different problem, and interacting with them all amounted to a lot of lost, depleted energy. No wonder Isadora lived in virtual isolation. At least in the mountains she had peace of mind.

Safe upstairs in her room, Morgana removed her clothes, pinned up her hair, then stepped into her shower. The hot water eased the tension that bore down upon her shoulders. After a while, she picked up her sponge, soaped it, and began scrubbing herself, hoping to wash away all the tension the party had created for her.

She knew that water was a precious commodity; yet, she allowed the shower to run much longer than usual, hoping it would cleanse her of the illness that still burned her organs as if bees were constantly stinging them. The stomach cramps came and left whenever she ate or drank anything. They left her weak and short of breath. No, she decided, it wasn't the people who had been enjoying the party that disturbed her. It was her inability to summon the necessary energy to cope with them.

Morgana finally turned the shower off and grabbed a towel to dry herself. As she bent down to dry her feet, a dizzy spell caused her to hold tightly to the towel rack. Must have been that drink, she thought. Could have been Kelly, too, she thought as she waited for the blackness to subside. There's something about him. Yes, I've overdone it tonight! I must get to bed. She slipped on her gown and put on her robe, then left the bathroom. She opened the top drawer to her chest, then hesitated a moment. Her senses told her that there was a strangeness in the room, one with which she was not familiar. She quickly turned toward the door—it was still bolted. No, she assured herself, there is nothing here. Still, she walked over to the door and relocked it. Then as she turned, she saw Eagle Eyes standing at the foot of her bed. "How did you get in here?" she demanded.

He smiled. "Through the open balcony door."

"But that's impossible! No one can climb up from the outside."

His laughter reflected his brilliant smile and white teeth.

"I climbed down from up there." He pointed to the roof.

Too exhausted to deal with him, she sat on the bed and waited for him to tell her what he wanted.

"You are still not well, I can see that." He sat facing her a moment, then inquired, "If I made you a drink, will you drink it?"

She raised her head to protest, but instead hesitated a moment, then looked him earnestly in the eye. "At this point, I will try anything. The pills the doctor gave me do nothing. It seems as though I am losing myself in this illness."

He rose, took a pillow and gently laid her back. Then he covered her with a blanket that she kept at the foot of the bed. "I'll be in the bathroom concocting your drink. He turned and left the room, leaving the door slightly ajar.

Morgana knew he wasn't officially a doctor. Yet, as she heard him tinkering with water and her porcelain cup, she wanted desperately to be well. Never in her whole life had she been so ill! Perhaps, she reasoned, it was because Isadora had always been there to protect her—body and soul! But now, Isadora was gone and this illness ransacked her body.

Eagle Eyes approached with the serenity of a light-footed fawn; then he sat beside her. "It will taste bitter, but you only need take a little. It will also make you rest." He looked away from her a moment, failing to add that it might also make her hallucinate, but he would remain with her until the danger was passed and she was resting. "You must remain absolutely quiet. Above all, relax. I have brought you some water to wash this down. It will help. I am positive." He took her hand gently and pulled her up into a sitting position, then handed her the cup. "Look at me when you drink it!" he ordered.

"Why?" she stammered, "is it a love potion?"

He laughed, "I wish that it were! You have an unusual sense of humor. I like that." He took her hand.

She sipped, then gagged as she forced the drink down, thinking to herself that, perhaps, she wasn't ill after all. Her eyes teared after her first sip of the drink, but he took her chin in his hand and forced her to face him.

"Drink, Morgana. I'll be here with you. If you don't drink, you'll get worse." He urged her on with a voice filled with understanding and sudden compassion. "I'll be here until you rest. Now, drink!"

Her eyes blurred from tears as the warm bitter liquid passed her throat, then filled her churning stomach. His hand was gently cradling her head, helping her hold the liquid down and stopping her from forcing it away. "Good!" he urged as he held her head tightly to encourage her to drink more. She struggled. He pinched her nose to make the drink go down her throat, but she cried out, allowing some of the brew to dribble out of her mouth. He quickly grabbed a towel to wipe her face.

"It's okay." With the glass of water, she rinsed her mouth, then wiped her lips. He thought she might throw up. "Rest now." He went to the bathroom to rinse the cup and upon hearing quiet sobs, he took his time rinsing out the towel, allowing her time alone. A sudden knock on the door stilled his movements. He dropped the towel and hid behind the bathroom door.

"*Hija*," her father called, "are you in bed?"

Morgana instantly sat up. The blanket that covered her fell to the floor. "Yes, Father." she answered as she wiped her eyes. "Coming!" She quickly unbolted the door and allowed him to enter.

"You okay, baby?" he asked, feeling her shake.

"Tired, that's all." she added, knowing full well that he was feeling very good from all the beer that he'd drunk. "How about you?"

"I feel terrific. It was a great party! Hey, it's cold in here. Let's close that window." He turned toward her. "What did you think about Kelly? Nice *hombre*. Rich, too. Never hurts to have some bucks, no?" He smoothed her hair. "But, I'm proud that you threw his necklace back in his face. Some of those guys like to take advantage of us!" he snickered.

"He's not from these parts, Father. You yourself told me," she added.

"Oh ... well. You don't have to take nothing from nobody, understand?"

She merely nodded. No use arguing with him, she thought, glancing apprehensively toward the bathroom door.

"Goodnight, *hija*. Rest well."

After he'd left, Morgana felt herself sway and leaned against the door for support. "Too much ... " She fainted.

Eagle Eyes knew the medicine was taking effect and hurried to catch her before she buckled to the floor. He easily carried her to her bed and laid her upon it. The door was not bolted and unsure whether her father would return or not, he decided to tend to that first.

He turned out the lights, then returned to her bed. The blazing New Mexico moon shone brilliantly through the sheer panels of the balcony doors, allowing him enough light to see that her eyes were closed. He covered her with a blanket, then went around to the window and looked out. The party lamps still glowed warm in the rustling wind. He relocked the window bolts, making sure he would not be interrupted, then returned to the bed and sat on its edge.

She was out cold. He dared not disturb her. It was enough that she was close by. He rose and walked slowly to the window and gazed out. After a while, he pulled up a chair and sat there thinking of how her father had planned well by putting her upstairs in a room sectioned off by itself. Her room was built in the highest section of the house, allowing just one entrance and one exit, but a nice balcony with double doors. A good form of protection, he thought, but not good enough to keep a smart Indian out.

His thoughts returned to Kelly. Kelly's curiosity about Morgana was unusual. Eagle Eyes had watched as Kelly followed Cruz around from person to person, but he had noted that Kelly's eyes had been on Morgana.

The man had a dark mystique about him, as if he were an investigative reporter or a shrewd detective.

A short time later he noticed that Morgana was still sleeping. He rose and touched her chin and brought her lips to his, then lightly kissed her. He played with her hair as if it were a tangle of feathers.

Much later he heard Morgana sigh. She stretched but did not wake.

The warmth Morgana felt made her desire nothing more than to hibernate like a fat bear on a cold night. At this moment, she craved sleep. The colors that exploded within her mind thrilled her. She felt as if she were floating through light clouds filled with brilliant stars.

He moved to sit on the edge of her bed. "You are beautiful, Morgana Cruz," he muttered feeling sudden closeness to her. "But, you must sleep and rest," he whispered. "You must get well." He held her wrist and counted her heartbeats, satisfied that she was okay. Sufficient time had passed for any hallucinations to have happened and he felt it safe to leave her.

Eagle Eyes noted her deep slumber, then glanced toward the window. There were faint traces of twilight showing through the balcony door. He gave her a soft kiss, then went to open the balcony door. He pulled down the rope he had used to lower himself, then climbed to the roof, and over the boulder that lay behind the house. Then he walked across the mountain, following a small overgrown trail leading to the other side of the mountain where he had parked his truck.

Chapter 8

Morgana woke with a start. The house was still. She glanced over at the clock on the night stand. It was one in the afternoon. Her father always slept late after a fiesta, and Marisol usually stayed in her weaving room. At times like these her father didn't bother to wake up to feed the horses, nor did Marisol fix breakfast as was her daily custom.

Her father would be very disappointed if he were to find out that she had allowed Eagle Eyes into her room even if nothing had transpired, except for that drink of herb tea which contributed to her feeling so good this morning. She decided that her father did not need to know a thing about the medicine she'd taken. It would be as much her secret as her *"Kinaalda"* was. She probably wouldn't see Eagle Eyes again, but last night he seemed different, more understanding and genuinely concerned about her health.

She rose and sensed herself well enough to go out. She would feed the horses, and she might even exercise La Luna. Morgana was sure La Luna was anxious to see her. She would walk the lively pinto at a leisurely pace.

The day was so clear that the Sandía peaks were highly visible. The temperature joyously hinted of the coming of winter. She walked hurriedly to the barn stopping only to admire the view of the mountains far in the distance. Seeking strength from their enormous boulders and peaks, she would ride toward the mountains

La Luna pranced playfully and tossed her head happily upon seeing Morgana, brushing against her to let her know that she had been missed. Morgana returned the strokes of affection with hugs and mutterings of endearment. Then she fed La Luna and the other horses.

La Luna shivered wildly when Morgana placed the saddle on her, knowing they were going for a long overdue ride. Morgana mounted the horse and they moved slowly out of the barn. Once she was settled in the saddle, La Luna hurried in the direction of the mountains they both loved.

The path Morgana chose was one she'd known since she was a child. It crisscrossed the ranch next to her father's and wasn't as treacherous as some of the others in the area. She knew of a secret spot—a spot that for her was near perfect. It was still undiscovered as it was on private property, property that she now remembered belonged to Kelly. She was sure Kelly wouldn't mind if she trespassed, so she spurred La Luna onward.

As she approached the spot, she found it cool—a slight mist was still lingering among the trees and brushes. Each step La Luna took upon the stones resounded with echoing vibrations, causing birds to flutter and small animals to scurry about the shaded area. The sound of the stream cascading down the rocks soothed Morgana, who immediately dismounted and walked to the water's edge. La Luna followed, dipped her head and drank freely. Morgana found her favorite rock and sat watching the velvety pinto drink, shaking herself with pleasure. No rattler would dare spoil the atmosphere here. Eagle Eyes, she thought, should see this heavenly place.

Eagle Eyes, whom she had disliked immensely during Isadora's burial ritual, was now someone she could like—given the chance. Yet, his need for being top commander scared her. She was not one to take orders and she— more than anyone else—realized how spoiled and sheltered she'd been all her life. Still, hadn't he commandeered himself into her fiesta, into her bedroom even, then given her an herbal drink? These things he did as an uninvited guest. Caution, she advised herself—take caution with Eagle Eyes.

She rose slowly, then pulled off her jacket, shirt and jeans and stepped naked into the cool waters. She waded out, knee deep, threw back her head, allowing her hair to get saturated with the refreshing water and to float along. Lazily she watched the clouds as they moved in one direction. The remedy Eagle Eyes had given her certainly boosted her energy and she felt great . . . renewed, refreshed enough to go back to her studio to prepare some unusual pieces for the coming holidays.

She laughed with delight upon feeling the slippery rocks beneath her feet, then dove deep and came up for air only when absolutely necessary. It was a small pond, no more than twenty feet wide, shaded by a tall ridge. The fish playfully nipped on her legs as if they were babies sucking on their bottle. Morgana happily enjoyed the moment, sensing that it might be a long while before she could return to the spot. Kelly now owned this land and she knew there was something about him that she'd not been able to identify. It would be best if she never came back.

Her playful frolicking and happiness suddenly disappeared as she thought of Kelly. She slowly stepped out of the water and walked to the trees where her clothes lay and she pulled them on. There, she sat in the sun, shaking out her hair, allowing it to fall loosely to dry. She closed her eyes and turned her face upward to the radiant sun thinking of Isadora and of a long time ago when she had been fourteen. At that time she had asked her wise master about love.

"What is love, Isadora?" She and Isadora had been riding, searching an isolated mountain for a particular clay.

"There are many kinds of love, girl. There is love between man's soul and Mother Earth. There is love between a man and his wife. There is love between a young brave and his young girl. Then there is love between friends. All these loves are different, but equally important."

She had seen that Morgana's head was bowed as if in shame.

"Love, all love, is a wondrous, beautiful thing. Know that and everything else will fall into place for you. There is no shame in love. There's shame only in not giving love when it is expected!"

She had taken Morgana's chin in her hand. "Love is as precious as water to dry land. Do you understand, my daughter?"

Morgana had sighed. "Yes, Isadora, but what is love like?" She had glanced up slightly at the old woman who had nodded that she had understood.

"I see what you mean." She had dismounted and had studied the sky a moment. "Come, let us sit here and rest." She walked to a rock surrounded by cactus and a tree. "Has your mother not spoken to you of these things?"

Morgana had sat next to Isadora. "No, she never has. It is like she is afraid and will not discuss it."

Isadora had frowned. "It still hangs upon her like a dark shadow. I hoped that she would have gotten over the situation."

"What situation do you speak about, Isadora?" Morgana had asked curiously.

"That will be up to your mother to tell you, but let me answer your question. The love act is one which depends a great deal upon your partner. For the girl is like a soft mare, unschooled yet trusting; and the boy, well, is like a stallion—eager—crazy for her and only aware of his strength and his desire to possess her. He will be master in the consummation of the act, for it is his position. When they come together as one for the first time, if he is considerate and takes care to soothe her fears and to woo her, she will not feel much discomfort. She will remember only the pleasurable feelings she receives." Isadora had studied the girl who had remained silent. "It is a natural act, my girl."

She had watched the girl turn away from her as if not caring to learn much more. Isadora had taken Morgana's hand to reassure her. "Do not fight the facts as I present them. If he is a good person, he will care for you, but there are men who are not caring and only want their immediate release. Then, when the girl is unprepared or not willing, it will indeed hurt her. Such a forceful act is called rape by the white man's law. Unfortunately, it is ignored by Indian law unless the father of the girl calls for revenge—which is rare." Isadora had spoken no more. She had waited for Morgana to absorb all she'd said.

When Morgana had finally broken the silence, she had said firmly, "Isadora, I shall never marry."

Isadora had laughed loudly. "You are young and innocent. Yes, you will marry, but that is many years away, long after you have finished college and long after you are master of the clay. Be happy for now. Live for today and leave tomorrow alone."

Now, many years later, Morgana smiled thinking of that past episode. "Yes, leave tomorrow alone!" she shouted to the trees and the mountain. She laughed loudly as Isadora had always laughed.

Eagle Eyes had strength and his power among the tribe certainly captivated her. She closed her eyes to recall the qualities and feelings she liked most—the smell of his skin so like a morning in spring, the roughness of his chin against her face and the soothing warmth of his hands that were like steel, yet, capable of gentle healing.

"Morgana!" a voice called.

The voice shattered her thoughts and her eyes flew open in apprehension. Then she saw Kelly standing several yards away.

"I'm sorry. I've frightened you," he added on seeing her bolt up.

"What are you doing here?" she asked angrily.

An amazed look crossed Kelly's face. "Sorry," he added firmly, "but I own this mountain. I could ask you the same question."

Morgana was shocked to see that La Luna was affectionately nuzzling Kelly's hair as if she'd known him for years. Was that why the horse had not warned her, she wondered. Of course, she quickly thought, La Luna had met Kelly while he was visiting with her father. Angrily, she whistled for La Luna who merely glanced her way.

"La Luna!" she called. "Come here!" The horse shook her mane but did not go to her mistress.

Kelly began to stroke the mare.

Morgana turned angrily to fetch her boots, but Kelly immediately said, "Don't go."

Morgana faced him, saying nothing, yet fiercely staring hard enough to cause Kelly some concern.

"Stay," he added softly. He removed his hat and slowly seated himself on a large rock, then rubbed the back of his neck, after which he glanced up hesitantly. "Will you have a seat?" He watched the struggle raging upon her face, sure that she would decide to leave that instant. "Give me a break, Morgana. Am I such an ugly guy?"

Morgana stared at him. "No, it's not that."

"Good then," he said, adding, "let's get to know each other." He pointed to a distant rock. "Sit over there, if you please."

She glanced at La Luna and then at the rock. "Only for a short while. I have to get back home."

He nodded and looked up at the sky. "It's a beautiful day, isn't it?"

She sat slowly on the rock and softly added, "Yes, it is."

He glanced at her. "Are you feeling better?"

She smiled. "I guess you can tell. How long have you been watching me swim?"

"I heard a horse coming and hid. I didn't know what or who to expect, so I did the logical thing and settled behind a boulder. After all this is my ranch. There should be no one on it at all except me."

"You are right. I was trespassing. This used to be the old Jackson place. When did you buy it?"

"A year ago, but I've only been out here for four months."

"My father didn't mention it to me. I thought it was still for sale."

"I bought it cheap. The strip mining almost destroyed it, but I think it can be salvaged."

"You are an ... Indian," she questioned, studying La Luna who stayed by his side.

"Yes ... Seminole from Oklahoma." He quickly looked down as if ashamed of his heritage. "But, I am a rich Indian, if that suits you. Many people don't like me. Many people have loved me. I am mostly just me."

She offered no comment for a while, then asked, "Are you married?"

"No, I was engaged once. We lived together for such a long time. We never married. My fault, I guess. Then she was killed. You see, she got angry at a party one night. I was acting the fool. She left the party without my knowledge and never came home. Four days later the police found her at the bottom of a cliff. My beautiful Ginny had been killed. The police have not found the murderers. When they do I'll kill them myself. I have the means to do it."

The anger in his voice caused Morgana to flinch and she was unable to speak.

"You see, Ginny made me rich. She was able to see things, to know things. Her intuition was phenomenal. She guided me through some deals that made me my money. Horse racing, dog races, buying and selling stock. I merely asked her what she thought and she answered. Then I followed her advice. Seldom was Ginny wrong. All she asked of me was that we marry. But, I didn't come through."

"When did this happen?" Morgana asked, leaning forward, straining to hear him because his voice grew softer.

"Five years ago ... ages ago ... a lifetime ago. I left Oklahoma and came out here seeking ... ." He stopped talking, rose and walked to the water's edge.

She watched his broad shoulders tighten and his fist twitch.

"She's everywhere I go. She never lets me sleep. There is no peace for me and it is the price I must pay for not marrying her. She will never allow me to forget ... ." Suddenly, he laughed hysterically. "And what's really strange is that I loved her so much. She kept insisting that we leave that damn party, but I wanted to continue gambling. She asked twice and then she was gone." He turned to Morgana. "If I had known the outcome of that night, I would have shut our doors and never left our house."

Morgana watched the tormented man from the rock where she sat. Finally, she said, "Isadora would say that you must rid yourself of her spirit. You must be cleansed and everything she owned must be burned. Then you will receive peace. That is the Navajo law. I am not Isadora. I feel that you must talk to Ginny's spirit of your love for her and pledge that her memory will be kept sacred. Let her know that you would have married her. Perhaps then, her spirit will live in peace."

He stared at her unbelievably. "Do you believe in such things? I do not. You see, I was reared by white people."

"Isadora, my master, taught me much, but I prefer not to use her teaching except in regards to pottery. You see, because my parents are of two different races, I have to blend in with both worlds in order to survive."

"I am Seminole. Ginny was Anglo. Her people saw her as very strange because of her psychic abilities."

Morgana rose. "I have to go."

He is not bad looking, she thought, but he is big. He has the physique of a full-back on a major football team. Yet, I do see the Indian in him—his nose and his slightly slanted eyes offer hints of his heritage. Then there's that patch. She thought of Eagle Eyes, of his hot skin and his cool approach in all matters.

"I didn't mean to tell you all that about Ginny. It just tumbled out of my mouth. I am a wizard in business matters, but where women are concerned, I seem to be forever stumbling. I apologize." He studied her for a moment.

"Kelly, I need to go." She rose from the rock and pushed her hair out of her face.

He continued as if he had not heard her. "Your father is a grand person ... I am glad we've become friends. I feel I could trust him and you. I saw that when you returned the necklace."

Morgana added, "I don't want your necklace."

Kelly immediately said, "Yes, I know that."

She moved toward La Luna, then stopped. "How did you meet my father?"

Kelly stroked La Luna's head. "He wandered into my campsite one night, looking for strays. I remember his hair shone like silver in the early hours of twilight. Those green eyes of his were fierce like a lion's. The next thing that caught my attention was that his silver beltbuckle had diamonds that formed a 'C.' He wasn't frightened of me. He didn't have a gun or a rifle. All he wanted was his lost cattle. After some clumsy introductions, I invited him to coffee and we shared some fried fish. The next day we herded the cattle over to your place." He moved around to Morgana's side. "I saw you on the balcony. Your hair was shining like black gold."

"I see," she added, taking the reins.

"I thought of my mother when I saw Cruz. He would have been ideal for her."

"What do you mean by that!" Morgana asked.

"Mother called me "Kindle Who Stirs Up Blazes." He moved to another rock and stood as memories of his mother and the way she suffered rushed through his mind. "My mother was Seminole. She would take me up to a pond and we would swim and eat our lunch. She was a simple woman who loved the wrong man. A man who gave her nothing but illusions, poverty and pain. In my own mind, I would have preferred for her to have loved someone as strong as your father. She would have been happier. I also would have been happier."

He turned and with two giant strides, he closed the gap between them, seizing her in a tight grip and flinging her up into his arms. He started spinning and swirling her around playfully.

"Stop it!" she screamed.

He continued swirling her as if she were on a merry-go-round. She held tightly to his neck for fear of his letting her go. Then, she became dizzy as they went round. His breathing became labored and when he finally was unable to stand, he fell with her into the cool water, where he immediately released her, allowing her to move on her own. He roared with laughter like a crazy happy bear flopping gaily.

Morgana watched stunned. This was not the same serious businessman that she'd seen with her father. He seemed crazy, like a kid with a new toy. Still, she felt the need to be on the alert, even though it was obvious that he had released a tremendous amount of tension by this uncharacteristically playful act. She treaded water and silently watched as he flipped around in the water much like a tremendous whale anxious to submerge and re-emerge, making unbelievable waves that rushed to the bank.

"The water is not that deep! Be careful! There are rocks beneath us!" she screamed.

She wondered if he had heard her. Her skin prickled a warning. A sense of fear sparked by an urge to get out of the water flashed over her. She turned to move to the bank, took several steps, then glanced back. She saw that he had not emerged from his last dive.

"Kelly!" she screamed, alarmed that something was not right. La Luna neighed, complaining vigorously and nervously prancing in and out of the water. She too was on alert. Morgana searched the bank. No! He had not surfaced! She quickly dove head first into the water. His frolicking had so muddied the water that it was hard for Morgana to see. She surfaced, then swam farther in to dive deeper. She surfaced once again and scanned the water. Still, he had not surfaced. She dove deeper this time and found him. The back of his shirt was fastened to a tree branch that penetrated from the rocks below.

She frantically worked with both hands to tear the shirt away. His body drifted upward and she was thankful that the water made him weightless. The water hole she knew was no deeper than twenty feet, yet for someone who did not know it as well as she, it could be treacherous, filled with hidden rocks and crannies that needed gentle exploring.

She gasped for needed air when she surfaced, then turned her attention to Kelly, whom she managed to tug to the bank. Unable to pull his body any further, she called for La Luna who responded instantly and stood patiently at her side, waiting for her orders. She took the rope that was fastened to her saddle and tied it to Kelly's arm.

"Move back, La Luna," she cried. "Move slowly."

The horse, sensing the urgency in Morgana's voice, pulled the man safely to a clump of grass and weeds. There La Luna stopped. Morgana quickly untied the rope, stopping only to see the horrendous scar that covered his bad eye. She kept staring at Kelly's eye, then turned him on his side, causing the water to fall from his mouth and nose. Not much residue came out so she shoved his stomach with pressure from her bare foot forcing the water to spurt out.

Kelly lay unconscious before her. She decided to shove with her foot once again. More water let go its hold from his lungs. She pushed him upon his back and began blowing air into his mouth, counting to five, then breathing into his lips once again.

A spasm overtook his large frame which caused him to roll on his side and jerk. His eye flipped open, yet it seemed sight-less, veiled with a heavy, far away look which made it seem dull and uncaring. His other eye was missing.

"Kelly!" she called anxiously, but his response chilled her more than his missing eye. His functioning eye slowly closed, as she took his left wrist to check his pulse. It was there, but moving slowly. She reached up to the saddle and pulled down a blanket. At least he was breathing. She must get help!

She gathered some dry twigs and leaves to put around him, then covered him with the blanket. "I'm going to get Father! Kelly, do you hear me! I'm going to get Father to help you!" Satisfied that it was the best she could do for him, she stood up and mounted La Luna, spurring her onward in a fast gallop toward the ranch.

The evening shadows would be falling soon. Morgana was chilled, yet she encouraged La Luna to hurry on without giving her a moment to rest. Soon it would be nightfall and it would get much colder.

The trail was treacherous in some parts and she had to slow her horse down to a careful pace. The last thing she wanted was to injure La Luna. She patted La Luna affectionately on getting through a narrow section between two large cliffs. "Good girl," she muttered. Once the land cleared, she shot down the valley as fast as she could, shivering each time her long tangled hair slapped more moisture upon her back. "Father will know what to do!" she assured herself as she clenched her teeth, forcing them to quit chattering. She raced on. Soon, she sensed, if she did not change into warm dry clothes, she would be terribly ill again.

The ranch house came into view. "Bless the spirits for those lights!" she uttered loudly. She bent forward as close as possible to La Luna's head, whispering encouragement to her. As soon as they flew past the barn, she started pulling back on the reins.

"Father!" she yelled as she reached the door that led to the kitchen. She pulled the horse to a halt. "Father!" she called again as she dismounted and opened the door.

Frank Cruz hurried through the kitchen, a worried look on his face. He'd never heard his daughter scream in such distress. He gasped in horror upon seeing her drenched and shivering. "Marisol!" he yelled. "Come here quick!"

"Father!" Morgana cried, "Kelly is up on the ridge at the water hole. His shirt got caught and he didn't come up. I pulled him out, but he wasn't breathing. I did CPR and he started breathing, but he's unconscious. He needs help quickly!"

"Marisol, get her dry!" Cruz commanded as he rushed to the phone to call the emergency number used by rural residents in the high sierras.

"Father, I might have broken his rib. I had to use my foot as a lever to get his lungs free of water." Morgana was near Cruz's shoulder, pulling on him and speaking hurriedly to him. She was unaware that Marisol was pulling her the other way, trying to get her attention. "Father, he's probably dead by now!"

"Marisol!" Cruz yelled. "Get her out of here!"

Marisol, knowing that Morgana was in shock, yanked her daughter towards her, then slapped her across the face. The blow stunned Morgana, who instantly stopped her incessant yelling and started to cry. Marisol put her arm around her and quickly led her upstairs to her room.

Chapter 9

Cruz informed the emergency rescue team of the exact location of the waterhole. They would fly out in a helicopter. If he worked quickly, he thought, he could even reach Kelly precious moments before the helicopter did, thus allowing him time to light a fire to pinpoint the spot where Kelly lay unconscious or possibly dead.

He rushed to the barn where he pulled out a large flashlight, rope, and extra blankets, into which he placed two logs with which to start a fire. It took him a few moments to saddle his stallion, Santos. He pulled out "Lucky One," his sharp shooter rifle, and filled his pockets with ammunition. No telling what he might find up in the mountains this time of night. The last thing he wanted was to meet a mountain lion and God help Kelly if one had already picked up his scent!

He mounted Santos. The stallion danced a few fancy steps to let Cruz know that he was ready for this adventure, then snorted eagerly as he dashed out of the barn on command. The excited stallion moved quickly.

Cruz spurred Santos on until they reached a point where the high boulders almost touched shoulder to shoulder. The stallion eased his way through the tight-fitting passageway with as much grace as a well-schooled Spanish stallion. Cruz smiled triumphantly, pleased with his mount. He eased Santos through the last tight crevice into a clearing. The full moon served as a lamplight, helping Santos dodge the Palo Verde trees and clumps of cedars that dotted the mountainside.

As expert a horseman as Cruz was, he had a problem with his eyes which failed him in the luminous light. Shadows which came and went, then did a quick disappearing act, caused him to wipe his eyes frequently.

He cursed, admitting to himself that age had crept up on him. His thoughts turned to Kelly. Somehow, he felt a keen friendship with the man, but what was he up to? Was Kelly's meeting a chance encounter with Morgana? Could he have staged it? Impossible! How would Kelly have known she would be riding today?

Morgana knew the territory as did her horse, La Luna. Cruz knew the waterhole well, for he'd taken Morgana there many times as a child. They would swim together until he'd gotten too busy with the cattle to go swimming. He missed the closeness he'd treasured with his daughter when she was a little girl. Now, as a woman, she seemed remote, distant, seeking her place in strange places and with different people like Isadora. This annoyed him! Why couldn't things remain constant, never changing?

His thoughts made him remember the first time he had met Isadora, *la bruja*, the witch, as he called her. At that time, he had been trying hard to please Marisol and had weakly consented to meeting the Indian woman. Marisol had led him blindfolded to Isadora's hogan where his bandana had been taken off. He had sat cross-legged directly across from Isadora, rendered speechless by the image of the old woman who sat before him. Her face was filled with wrinkles that twitched in every direction and she scared the pants off him. An ancient relic that should have been put out of misery long ago, he thought. But, he swallowed his fears and stared boldly at the old woman as she threw something into the fire in front of them, causing him to jump away from her.

"Don't be alarmed!" she had ordered, never removing her eyes from his face. "I know that in your heart you are a good man, but even more important, I see your love for Marisol is true." Isadora had nodded knowingly. Cruz glanced lovingly at Marisol, who had kept her head bowed as if ashamed. "A child shall come unto both of you ... a beauty she will be ... a blessing to all of us ... but not until you both have learned much about each other. Beware, Cruz, mend your ideas and try not to class people in categories. Accept all people regardless of skin color or their stations is life. Be kind to them. Hear me!"

Cruz had glanced at the old woman over the smoldering fire. Witch, he had wanted to scream! He had forced himself to remain quiet, keeping his eyes on the fire, until the session had been complete. When it was over, he rose and let Marisol blindfold him once again. He let her lead him away from the hogan and out of the reservation, vowing never to return. Still, he now felt as he rode along, that the visit had carved battle lines between him and Isadora.

Santos galloped on fiercely. Crusts of salt covered his velvety chest. "A little further, Santos," muttered Cruz gently. He searched for the helicopter which he knew should be coming upon them soon. He heard nothing but the frantic beating of Santos's hooves and the stallion's labored breathing.

The crescent-shaped moon peeked behind dark ominous clouds as Cruz began the last climb to the plateau. Santos neighed, smelling the nearby water as he slowed his pace.

"*Ándale, Santos*. Hurry on!" urged Cruz as he tightened his grip, letting the stallion know that time was of the essence. Cruz pulled out his large flashlight. Yards ahead lay the waterhole. As the horse hurried onward, he flashed the light, frantically searching from left to right, hoping to find Kelly.

"Kelly!" he yelled, expecting a response. Getting none, he dismounted and pulled out his rifle. He proceeded to walk around the outskirts of the waterhole, flashing the light among fallen tree trunks and clumps of boulders.

Santos suddenly snorted, did a fast challenging dance, then reared up on his hind quarters. Cruz turned quickly and flashed the light on the horse.

"Is he nearby, Santos?" Cruz questioned the horse, aware of the stallion's alarm.

The stallion galloped up to Cruz, then flicked his head angrily. Cruz continued to move forward, searching the dark bank. "Kelly?" he yelled. "Man, where are you?"

Cruz was at a loss as to where to look. Proceeding slowly, he neared the site where Morgana had said she'd left Kelly. It was Santos who walked over to smell the fallen man.

"Kelly! *¡Hombre!* My God!" Cruz fell to his knees, put down his rifle and positioned the flashlight so that it shone upon the stricken man.

Kelly's forehead was oozing dark liquid that ran freely down the side of his face. His body felt cold to the touch. Cruz turned to Santos to fetch the extra blanket he'd brought. He covered Kelly, then fetched his wood. He needed to start a fire. Suddenly, he heard the chopping sounds of the coming helicopter which filled the canyons with vibrating echoes. As rapidly as he could, Cruz gathered fallen twigs and dropped to his knees to start the fire. The echoes resounded loudly in his ears, but as he glanced upward he failed to see the CARE helicopter.

He cursed as his match failed to light. He repeated the process, only to fail once again. "Curse hell!" he howled, as the fire started to smoke. He blew on the small flame and failed to notice that Santos pranced vigorously back and forth snorting in an alarmed manner. The horse finally dashed around the outskirts of the waterhole, neighing loudly.

Cruz bent over Kelly seeking signs of life. Santos reared then and flew past Cruz into the darkness and security of the pine trees that surrounded the water hole.

Cruz grabbed Kelly by the shoulders and shook him vigorously in a desperate attempt to pull him from unconsciousness. "Kelly! Wake up! Help is here!"

The wind created by the chopper blades flung bits and pieces of sand and pine needles into the air. "Get up!" Cruz demanded as he continued to shake Kelly. It was hopeless. He stood up and frantically flashed his light toward the hovering helicopter, trying to attract their attention in order to direct them to the exact spot. "Here!" he yelled as he swung his arm in a continuous circle. "Over here!"

It took only a few seconds for the crew to spot the swirling light. The pilot quickly turned the spotlight upon the frantic old man below.

The medical attendants glanced down, wondering what was happening on the ground below. They had been informed to look for a possible drowning victim. All they could see was a man waving a flashlight. The helicopter slowly came down, but then the pilot yelled and the helicopter wavered uncontrollably from side to side as the pilot spotted a large brown bear with claws that gleamed in the brightness of the spotlight. The bear was standing directly behind the man.

The large animal hesitated only a second, then he embraced Cruz tightly, swinging him back and forth like a broken doll, all the while staring up at the bright spotlight from the chopper. Angered by the noisy intrusion, the bear dragged Cruz several feet out of the light.

The pilot quickly pulled the chopper to a safe distance away, ordering the crew to prepare for two possible emergencies. "Bring me the rifle!" the pilot ordered as he turned on the radio frequency to warn headquarters of the situation. "We have a problem with pickup," the pilot stated into the mike. "What is happening down there?" he asked, not believing his own eyes.

The pilot watched as another man struggled to sit up, then picked up a rifle, which he pointed at the bear still holding the old man. A rapid succession of shots were fired. The bear let Cruz go as if he were a discarded bone, then lunged at the man with the rifle. More shots were fired and the bear fell directly upon Kelly, who collapsed unconscious.

Unsure of whether the bear was dead or not, the pilot waited a long while before landing the chopper in a small clearing, yards away from the bloody scene. He allowed his crew to disembark to render aid to the two men below. The pilot stood on guard outside the chopper while the crew helped Cruz and Kelly.

"Hurry! Get them aboard! I don't like it up here!" the pilot yelled, anxious to get off the mountain!

After the stretchers were secured on the helicopter, the pilot radioed their arrival time. In seconds, the flying machine was off, slicing through the darkness of the crisp chilly night toward the safety of the Albuquerque hospital where a team of surgeons waited to receive them.

♡   ♡   ♡

A riderless Santos galloped to the back door of the Cruz kitchen and kicked at the wooden door, then neighed angrily.

Marisol peered out the window, then cried, "Santos! Where is the old man? Santos!" she shouted as the horse shook his head at her and snorted.

Marisol knew better than to approach the skittish animal. She reached for the phone to dial the neighboring rancher, but no one answered. She quickly called her cousin Tom Crooked Leg, asking him to come over immediately. Explaining the fearful situation as best she could, she then ran upstairs to Morgana.

"Daughter! Something has happened to your father! Santos is back without him!"

Morgana, dressed in a pair of jeans and a sweater, emerged from her bathroom. She paled. "Oh, no!" She rushed to the balcony to look below. The stallion was rearing furiously, angrier than she'd ever seen him. She ran downstairs, grabbed a coat, then took off to the barn, ignoring her mother's pleas to return.

Santos lashed out at Marisol as she emerged out the back door screaming after Morgana. The horse followed close on Morgana's heels to the barn. Morgana quickly saddled La Estrella, her mother's horse, and mounted her, hesitating long enough to grab a flashlight, then she tore out toward the mountain with Santos in the lead.

Images of her father flashed through her mind as she raced after the gallant horse whose hooves flung dust at them as he led the way. Let Father be okay, she prayed as they hurried past the shadowed prickly pear plants and the iridescent moon.

The stallion was waiting at the dark waterhole when Morgana and La Estrella arrived. "Papa!" she called. The stillness of the night air sent chills up her spine as she peered through the dark crevices and shadows, waiting for her father to respond.

"Kelly!" she called out as she stood high in her stirrups, searching among the clumps of jumping cholla and flashing her light well into familiar crevices and rock boulders. She saw nothing, but the odor of a rancid stench nauseated her immediately and sent the two edgy horses into an immediate alert.

"Easy there, La Estrella," she softly commanded as she hurriedly dismounted. She tied La Estrella to a nearby Palo Verde tree, knowing full well that the fidgety horse would bolt and flee at the least provocation.

Morgana walked cautiously to the spot where the beam from her flashlight reflected a silvery object. On bended knee, her hands shaking uncontrollably, she bent down and recognized Lucky One, her father's rifle, lying haphazardly upon the ground. Empty shells lay in close range. Her heart beat frantically as her hand seized the barrel of the Winchester. Nothing could part her father from Lucky One except death.

"Father!" she yelled loudly. She moved anxiously among the loose dirt and clumps of grass. "Good God!" she shrieked when she caught sight of the huge mass of brown fur that lay before her with its mouth opened in frozen agony.

Her piercing scream caused Santos to bolt upwards, his hoofs flying protectively to defend her. Like a sizzling bolt of lightning, he pounced upon the dead bear. The stallion's hooves sliced repeatedly into the sticky hairy mass of flesh, spattering Morgana with clumps of blood and tissue. At last, satisfied that he'd taken revenge for his master's disappearance, Santos halted his death dance.

Morgana fainted cold upon the ground. The blood-coated stallion neighed his displeasure, nuzzling her hair in an effort to wake her but a soft call from the mare, La Estrella, interrupted him. He slowly walked over to La Estrella to comfort her. After a few moments, the stallion left the mare and entered the water to cleanse himself of the bear's bloody remains.

Chapter 10

Tom Crooked Leg, accompanied by an angry Eagle Eyes, stopped his jeep at the foot of the sierra, then pointed his rifle upwards to the top plateau where the waterhole lay.

Tom Crooked Leg, a Vietnam veteran, with grey streaking his plaited braids, said, "I can't make it up with this bum leg, Eagle Eyes. Lucky for you that we were drinking tonight. Now you have the privilege of climbing up that mountain." He glanced over at Eagle Eyes whose jaw was set tight. "Loosen up, Eagle Eyes. So the girl was stupid to go up there at night—but it has happened, so let it be."

Eagle Eyes zipped up his jacket to ward off the chilly wind that whistled around them; he glanced at Tom Crooked Leg but did not respond.

Tom Crooked Leg jumped onto the hood of the jeep. "I've known you long enough to know that when those brown eyes of yours turn red, I stay out of your way. But, my favorite cousin, Marisol, is greatly distressed over her daughter and her husband. So I have to rely on you to help her out. Look yonder, the path is between the two highest peaks. Follow it and you will encounter the old waterhole. I shall wait here. If there is a problem, fire your gun once to signal me and I will radio for more help."

"Will do, Tom," Eagle Eyes replied with reluctance. "Stay close!"

Eagle Eyes started upward, then hesitated when Tom said, "I'll leave my jeep lights on."

Eagle Eyes started up the cliff, cursing to himself over the disruption of his planned evening. He did not particularly care to play at rescuing this girl-in-distress on such a cold night. A picture of Singing Waters flashed through his mind. She spoke in a soothing way and this cooled his anger in minutes. Morgana offered no peace, though she was more beautiful than Singing Waters.

He lost his balance on a rock and fell against the boulder. He rose and moved forward much more carefully, glancing below at the place where Tom Crooked Leg sat waiting. Eagle Eyes smiled as he waved at his friend, thinking that the only thing Tom Crooked Leg did well was to paint overpriced pictures for tourists. He was a simple man and he needed nothing else.

Eagle Eye's hands were cold when he reached the waterhole. The beam of Morgana's flashlight caught his immediate attention. He stood a moment to listen. Nearby he saw the stallion whose ears were pointed high, alert on seeing the stranger enter the area. Eagle Eyes sent the stallion a soothing call. He walked toward the flashlight and immediately fell on his knees before the unconscious blood-spattered Morgana.

The air smelled of death. His brown eyes widened as he quickly surveyed the area. His light flashed upon the remains of the bear, but he quickly turned his attention back to Morgana. A quick examination proved that she was uninjured. The danger lay in the scent of the blood that surely would attract other animals, possibly other bears. It was urgent that he get her away quickly. He carried Morgana to where the horses stood, but the stallion reared in objection. Eagle Eyes spoke to him gently, giving the stallion his freedom by choosing the mare to mount. Effortlessly, he threw Morgana over his shoulder, then mounted La Estrella. The stallion, he knew, would follow at a respectable distance and would warn him of other animals around. As a precaution, he felt for his gun. Morgana's father was not to be seen anywhere, but if he was in this area the stallion would have led Eagle Eyes to him. He moved slowly down the mountain, glad that Tom Crooked Leg waited below in his jeep.

He glanced down at Morgana, whose face rested angelically against the rough army jacket Tom Crooked Leg had tossed at him when they had left the warm hogan.

He cautiously glanced around. The stallion still followed. All I need now is to have another bear appear, too, and then we'd both be in a big mess, he thought. What adventures you cast my way, beautiful Morgana. He smiled to himself, then protectively clutched her still tighter. The snow would soon coat the high mountains for months. But for now, this razor sharp wind was enough to send the little party quickly tumbling down the mountain.

A sigh of relief escaped the cold lips of Eagle Eyes when he reached the jeep. He slowly dismounted and walked to the jeep with Morgana in his arms.

"Tom!" he called, as he peered into the jeep and saw that Tom was snoring loudly. Eagle Eyes placed Morgana in the jeep and covered her with another blanket, then went around to tie La Estrella to the rear of the jeep. Ordinarily, he'd leave the horses together, but it was much too cold for the smaller mare. The stallion would follow if he chose to. As he started the jeep, Morgana moaned and moved her head, then sat upright screaming.

"Father!"

Tom Crooked Leg bolted awake.

Eagle Eyes reached over and embraced her. "It's okay, it's okay!" he repeated.

Her eyes were wild. She blinked several times before she recognized him. "Did you find my father?" she cried desperately, trying to get free from the blanket.

"Listen to me!" He put his hand under her chin and turned her face to his. "He wasn't there. We'll look tomorrow, okay?"

"I agree with Eagle Eyes, Morgana," added Tom Crooked Leg. "I'm sure the old man is okay." He re-arranged the blanket around him and closed his eyes to sleep.

"We're going back to the ranch now." Eagle Eyes forced her to sit back in the seat. He put the jeep in gear, glanced back only once to make sure the mare followed and the pace was suitable for her. He noticed that the stallion did not follow.

As he drove, Eagle Eyes could see that Morgana was studying him. This made him uneasy, so he remained silent and concentrated on his driving.

"He isn't your father, so you wouldn't care," she cried. "We should go back!"

A lump in Eagle Eyes throat prevented him from answering. Yes, he thought, I had a father once who didn't care. One who wouldn't have gone after me. One who lived only for himself. One who had no love for me, as you obviously do for yours. But me, I was desperate for any love he threw my way like a starved young wolf hoarding each bread crumb. "Morgana, please ... " he began.

She turned on him, her anger flashing like that of a furious fighting cock. "Go back!" she demanded.

He stopped the jeep, then turned toward her, hesitating to collect his defense, then merely said, "No."

She caught her breath, then began to beg him, clutching his arm tightly, "Please, oh, please, go back."

Tom Crooked Leg also started to suggest they go back, but Eagle Eyes quickly turned to him. "No, it's too cold out there!" Thereupon, Tom Crooked Leg said nothing more.

"We will not go back! I have spoken!" Eagle Eyes stated.

Morgana settled back. She buried her face in the blanket and silently wept.

The rest of the trip was made in silence except for Tom Crooked Leg's occasional snore.

When they reached her house, Morgana bolted out the door and ran inside. "Mother!" she called, "where are you?" In the kitchen she found a note taped to the phone which said that Marisol had gone to the hospital in Albuquerque where Frank Cruz and Kelly had been taken. Marisol stated that she didn't know their condition and suggested that Morgana ask Cousin Tom to drive her there.

Morgana turned to run out the door, but found Eagle Eyes standing there waiting. "Well?" he questioned.

"I have to go to the hospital in Albuquerque. Tom can drive me."

Eagle Eyes laughed. "Tom's asleep."

She frowned. "Then I'll take the truck."

He reached over and took her arm, then softly said, "Go shower and change and I'll take you to Albuquerque—understood?"

Morgana merely nodded, then hurried upstairs. She rushed through her shower, then she pulled on her jeans and a bright sweater.

"Okay, Eagle Eyes, I'm ready!" she said once she was dressed.

Instead of going to the door, she went to the balcony and carefully opened the doors. But when she peered down, she saw neither Eagle Eyes nor Tom. "They must be in the living room," she thought. "Here's my chance to get going by myself."

She pulled a knotted rope out from under her bed, a rope her father had taught her to use in case of a fire. One end she secured to an iron hook he'd welded in place. The rest of the rope went over the balcony and down the edge.

Morgana glanced down below. This was a feat she had not practiced in a long while. She took a deep breath and heaved herself over the railing. Her hands burned and one of her shoulders popped as she continued to slide downward until at last she was safe on the ground. She smiled triumphantly, then shot past the entrance of the house and down toward the barn where the truck was parked.

The spare set of keys was in the barn on a hook near the tack room. She had only to get them and she'd be off! She tiptoed to the barn and peeked inside. Tom Crooked Leg was asleep on some bales of hay. La Luna looked over at Morgana and shook her mane excitedly. Morgana crouched low. Her plan was to steal past Tom Crooked Leg without waking him, then to get the keys and be off. Morgana quickly moved to the small tack room. She silently removed the keys, then turned to leave. Suddenly, she heard Eagle Eyes' voice. Hurriedly she moved behind a chest.

"Tom, my friend, wake up. I am going to take Morgana to Albuquerque. Please stay and take care of the place until I return."

Morgana dared not move. With Eagle Eyes in the barn, it would be too risky to leave. She decided to wait.

Tom sat up, rubbed his eyes and said, "Eagle Eyes, you hadn't told me you knew my little cousin."

Eagle Eyes chose not to say anything. He caressed La Luna's mane as Tom continued speaking.

"You two certainly get under each other's skin." He laughed. "Ah, love," he sighed happily. "It's grand!"

"You should try falling in love sometime, my friend. It might suit you."

"Oh, never!" added Tom as he threw a blanket over La Luna. "It's not for me! Oh, but little cousin is pretty as was her mother, something your father well knew. But, that's another love story from the past."

"My father was a cruel man." Eagle Eyes said as he faced Tom with eyes flashing red. "You know that."

Tom nodded. "Yes, but only after Marisol and he were not able to marry. Before then, he was as gentle as a fawn. Then all hell broke loose when he was forced to marry another girl." He hesitated a moment with his arm flung over La Luna's rump.

"Are you sure that Bold Feather did not father Morgana? The women of the tribe always said Marisol was pregnant when she married the Mexican. Perhaps you two are brother and sister?"

Eagle Eyes frowned but he said nothing.

Tom continued. "Lots of talk at that time. They also say Marisol went a little crazy after your father married. It's sad that no one bothered with her except Isadora. Then Cruz came along."

Eagle Eyes quickly interrupted him. "This is not your business."

"So be it!" Tom added, "but I'd find out more before getting involved any deeper." The blanket that he held slid over the mare. Tom reached across the animal's chest to secure it, and Eagle Eyes bent over to help him.

Morgana waited for the men to leave the barn. "It could not be!" she thought. "Is it possible we are half brother and sister?" She opened the door of the barn as quietly as she could and slid outside.

She saw the two men as they walked slowly toward the house. Once they were safely inside, Morgana moved to the patio and peeked in through a window. She did not see them, so she quietly entered the foyer and sat on a chair to wait. Is it possible that I'm not my father's child, she thought? No, he would not have allowed it. Had Isadora known anything about this affair? Surely, she must have known. She rose and paced the hallway.

Eagle Eyes and Tom each carried a cup of coffee as they returned from the downstairs kitchen.

"Let's go!" she ordered as she rushed out to the truck without waiting for them.

Eagle Eyes drove to Albuquerque while Tom slept and Morgana wrestled silently with the troubling thoughts bombarding her mind. Eagle Eyes drove carefully and in less than two hours they managed to reach the hospital.

The truck pulled to a stop directly in front of the hospital. Morgana disregarded Eagle Eyes's warning to be careful and jumped out. She rushed into the lobby and immediately asked where she could find her parents.

The Intensive Care Unit was to the right, the receptionist said, and Morgana hurried down the long hallway, wishing the white fluorescent lights weren't so bright. It was near midnight and she felt as if she hadn't slept in three days.

"Mother!" she called upon seeing Marisol sitting pathetically in the corner chair of the small ICU waiting area. She rushed over to her and the two embraced. "How is Father?"

"Sit, daughter," she said, then peering down the hall she asked, "Where's Tom?"

"He is coming, Mother. He's with Eagle Eyes. They'll be here shortly. Tell me about father!" she insisted.

"The bear that attacked your father lacerated his chest, tore up his lungs and he's just near torn to shreds. They don't know if he'll make it." Marisol wept into her hands.

Morgana hugged her, muttering, "How awful!"

Marisol nodded and wiped her nose before continuing. "I can't believe this. Kelly has a bad concussion and some water in his lungs. They had to stitch up several cuts as well. It was Kelly who shot the bear. If not for Kelly, your father would surely be dead and Kelly, also."

"Can I see Father?" Morgana asked almost in a whisper.

Marisol shook her head. "Not now, but you can see Kelly. He's in room 201. Thank him for me, daughter." She clutched her daughter's hand, then sighed deeply. Morgana hugged the woman who now seemed small and helpless. What else? thought Morgana. What else is expected of us?

Heavy sounds of boots raging upon the tile floor caused both women to look up into the angry eyes of Eagle Eyes. Morgana stood straight and defiant while Marisol rushed to embrace Eagle Eyes. She buried her tear-stained face in his chest, muttering how grateful she was he'd come.

Eagle Eyes embraced Marisol. After watching them for a moment, Morgana walked down the hallway to Kelly's room, leaving Eagle Eyes to comfort Marisol.

The door to Kelly's room was closed. She hesitated, took a deep breath, then entered. Kelly was awake, staring out the only window in the room. His dark eye seemed to light up as he saw her walk toward his bed. He reached out and took her hand.

"Kelly, you saved my father. I owe you for that. How do you feel?" she asked, glancing up at his forehead which was covered with white bandages. Then she glanced at his scarred eye, his eternal brand.

He reached up and touched his scar, ashamed to have it so visible. "I guess bears and I do not get along. It should be a lesson for me. And, I'll learn to stay away from waterholes."

"If not for you, my father would be dead," she added softly.

"And without your help, I'd be dead, too." He squeezed her hand. "Thank you."

Morgana reached down and kissed his cheek, closing her eyes to the dreadful scar. She saw a tear stray from his good eye.

"My mother and I always swam in a pond like that. I really got excited when I found out that such a beautiful spot could be on the land that I now owned. I had no idea it was there and just happened to stumble upon it."

Morgana remained silent a moment before saying, "I see."

"Is Cruz going to make it?"

She shook her head, "I don't know yet. Mother is very upset and I haven't seen the doctor. But Father will make it. He's strong and stubborn, too." She took his hand and kissed it. "Get some rest. I'll stop by later." She walked slowly to the door then waved at him as she quietly closed the door, then leaned against the wall and sighed. She hurried back to the ICU lobby.

Eagle Eyes paced back and forth like a caged hawk. He bolted forward on seeing her. "Where have you been?" he asked. Ignoring his question she replied with a question of her own, "Where is Mother?"

"She's with your father."

She walked toward the nurses' station and got the attention of a nurse. "May I see my father, Frank Cruz?" she asked.

The nurse looked through a glass partition, then back at her. "I'm afraid you'll have to wait. Mrs. Cruz is in there now and only one visitor at a time is permitted."

Eagle Eyes took her elbow. "Come with me!" He led her toward a vacant stairway leading out of the hospital.

Morgana felt the pinch of his fingers as they pressed roughly into her skin.

"Didn't you think about how your mother would have felt if you'd broken you leg by jumping out of the truck like that? Hasn't she endured enough pain without you possibly hurting yourself needlessly?"

She interrupted him. "You didn't think about that when you kidnapped me and took me up that mountain for Isadora's burial. I was gone three, almost four, days!" She tore herself free from his grip.

"That was a ceremonial ritual. It is commanded to be thus. I had no choice then."

"And what of my choices?" she raged. "I thought we were free to make our own decisions. Well, Eagle Eyes, I will decide my own destiny!" She pulled open the door to the hallway and hurried to the lobby.

Marisol emerged from the room and glanced from one to the other. She then raised her eyebrow in surprise. She'd never seen Morgana in such a huff, and Eagle Eyes looked as angry as a crazed bull.

Marisol smiled as she thought. So what is this I see between the son of my old friend and my daughter? Love has finally come to her after all these years. She surely will keep him on his toes forever, with him seeking and longing for her as would have happened between his father and me. Inwardly she smiled with satisfaction, then went to embrace them both lovingly. Morgana broke free from the embrace and entered the room where her father lay. Eagle Eyes lightly kissed Marisol's forehead. She heard him mutter in a saddened voice. "She's crazy!"

Marisol reached up and put her finger on his lips. "Please, be patient, my son." She added softly, "Yes, she is wild and untrained, but that is part of her beauty, is it not?"

"I'll get us come coffee, Marisol," he offered as he walked toward the cafeteria, rubbing the back of his neck as if he had a terrible migraine headache.

Chapter 11

Morgana stood at the foot of her father's hospital bed. Unprepared for the sight of her father connected to such unusual machines, she felt the blood draining from her face.

"Oh, Father!" she cried, feeling for him all the pain her eyes now revealed. "Can you hear me?" She took his bandaged hand in hers. "You're not going to die, are you? We have so much to do at home and we just won't let you go!"

Morgana sobbed, listening to the sounds that rang sharply from the machines next to his bed, sounds that indicated that he still was alive. She sat with him for a long time.

Daybreak was peeping through the windows. Nurses were coming and going. At last she knew she had to leave; she kissed her father on his forehead, then slowly left the room.

In the lobby, she found Marisol asleep, her head resting on Eagle Eyes' shoulder. He, too, was sleeping with his arms crossed securely across his chest. Morgana stared at both of them together and it seemed they had somehow struck a bond. His face, so peaceful in sleep, was finely sculptured; his nose, slightly angled downward; and his face, tanned by too many suns, was gilted, almost bronzed. His long, dark lashes secretly hid the golden brown eyes that flared up at the slightest anger. Could he be her half brother? She shook her head in disbelief, refusing to believe the conversation she'd overheard in the barn between Cousin Tom and Eagle Eyes.

"Mother," she called softly. Marisol woke with a start. She rose and rushed to Morgana. Eagle Eyes remained asleep.

"Daughter, how is your father?" Marisol asked, walking toward the door that led into the ICU. She reached for her handkerchief and blew her nose, gazing through the glass partition of the unit.

Morgana stood silent, observing the many emotions that played across her mother's face. Marisol was tired, crushed, and seemed unable to cope. "You okay, Mother?" she asked softly, trying to reassure her.

"It's awful hard seeing him like this. He is such a strong man—never allows anyone to help him. I'm afraid that he'll not make it and then I'll be lost without him to guide me." She bowed her head, letting her tears fall.

Morgana rushed to embrace her. "Lost? Never! You have me. We'll do fine. But, Papa is going to make it. He's a fighter, remember?"

Marisol squeezed her hand, then went to the side of her husband's bed.

Morgana returned to the lobby. Eagle Eyes was still asleep. He had not moved an inch. She watched him, feeling her anger build. She clutched her fists and hurried on to the cafeteria for coffee. When she returned with a cup of steaming coffee, he was gone. She looked in the ICU ward, but he was not there. Only Cousin Tom stood solemnly by the window in the corridor leading to the ward. She walked over to him.

Tom assured her that, given time, her father would recuperate. And she didn't have to worry about the ranch. He would feed the animals. "May the Great Spirit be with your father," he added as she hugged him.

And with me, she thought silently as she clung to him. She sighed, then walked back to the main entrance of the ICU ward.

She found Eagle Eyes staring at Marisol through the window of the ICU ward, watching as she gently held her husband's hand. His own hand he kept in a tight clasp over his belt buckle. His black Stetson was placed a little further back than usual. Worry lines creased his face.

She stood away from him and glanced helplessly at her father and mother, not daring to say a word lest she break down and cry.

Without glancing her way, Eagle Eyes thrust a paper at her. "I have reserved a room for Marisol and for you in the motel at the end of the block."

Morgana looked at the paper, then was ready to object, but he quickly turned, stood close to her and stated, "He will be here a long time. Tom and I will take care of the ranch. Stay as long as need be." He walked several yards away, then turned and added, "I will have Tom bring clothes for you both." Not waiting for an answer, he walked out of the hospital.

"Well," she added sarcastically, "don't bother to have an opinion, Morgana, he'll take care of everything." Why was she furious? She should feel grateful, but somehow she didn't feel that way.

Marisol crept silently up behind her. "What's this?" She looked at the paper in Morgana's hand.

"Eagle Eyes took the liberty of getting us a room at the motel across the way." She could not conceal the sarcasm in her voice.

"Oh!" Marisol beamed. "How thoughtful! He is so good. His thoughts are only for the good of others."

"Yes," added Morgana. "Such a good boy, almost like a son, right?"

"Yes," Marisol said softly. "A son whom ... "

Morgana pivoted and abruptly left the lobby to enter the ward where her father lay, leaving Marisol to wonder what her daughter could possibly have meant.

♡   ♡   ♡

For the next five days, Morgana and Marisol sat in shifts of six hours or more. If there was any emergency, one would immediately call the other. But the need to be constantly on the alert was taking its toll on them. Morgana began to fear losing both her father and her mother, for Marisol was definitely exhibiting signs of extreme fatigue and neuroses. Marisol's hands suddenly would not stop shaking, and she could not even hold a cup of coffee; constantly she complained about losing her way to the ICU ward. Morgana decided she would speak to the doctor about her mother when he came on duty later that night.

She herself had bitten her fingernails to the cuticle. Still, her father had not regained consciousness and Dr. Alonzo was not hopeful. He even had the audacity to tell them to go back to the ranch and wait there. Morgana knew she'd never leave her father until he got better, so the doctor's recommendation was meaningless.

Tom Crooked Leg came up every other day, but mostly he'd sit silently in the corner, staring down at his boots and speaking only to Marisol. He did not speak of Eagle Eyes nor had Morgana seen Eagle Eyes for the last five days.

Kelly came by in the morning of the fourth day. He was being discharged. "Morgana," he said as he took her hand, "if there's anything I can do, let me know." Into her palm he placed his business card with his phone number. She smiled up at him. "Thanks, Kelly. Right now ... well, I'll let you know."

Morgana watched him glance at his Rolex while another man she did not know joined him. They both hurried down the hallway as though they had a million things to do and no time to do them. He is really strange, she thought. She turned her attention back to her father.

The doctors and nurses quietly attended to their duties, ignoring Morgana's presence. Some were sympathetic, others were not, but she continued her vigil next to her father's bed, gently stroking his hand. "Father," she muttered quietly, "It's been days. Can't you give me a sign to show me that your soul is near? Blink your eyes, turn your head, or grip my hand. Please do something, Father."

She felt that he had not heard her, that his soul was traveling. In her mind, she imagined him as a young man, laughing joyfully, romping over the high snow-covered mountain tops. "Yes, Father, play for now, but you must return to me soon." She placed the crystal Isadora had given her on his chest, the sharp point aiming toward his mind's eye. No eyelash fluttered, no hand moved to grip hers, and there was no change in his breathing. As she stood silent, she suddenly decided to bring herself to ask Eagle Eyes for his help. Isadora was no longer around, but Eagle Eyes knew the secrets of healing. She would swallow her pride and ask him as soon as Marisol arrived for her shift.

"Miss Cruz, could you step aside?" Dr. Alonzo, a man in his late fifties, gently motioned her toward the hallway while he completed his examination. From the window, Morgana waited anxiously for her chance to speak to Dr. Alonzo about her father and about giving Marisol something to make her sleep.

She saw Dr. Alonzo peer deeply into her father's eyes. Afterward he stood silently reading the chart attached to the foot of the bed. He stood grim-faced, unhappily glancing at her father's face. Cruz should be conscious by now. He replaced the chart, then entered the hallway to speak to Morgana. "His condition hasn't changed. His vital signs are slow," he said as he nervously cleaned his eyeglasses, glancing down at her. "We'll wait a couple more days and then decide which route to take."

He turned to leave, but Morgana called to him, "Dr. Alonzo, it's about my mother. She's tired and can't sleep. She's disoriented. Will you please prescribe something for her?"

The doctor shook his head. "There is nothing she can really do here but work herself up into a frenzy. The best remedy for her is to remain at home."

Morgana shrugged her shoulders. "She won't go." He didn't bother to wait for her answer but entered the nursing station, where he concentrated on another chart. Morgana turned to see Marisol enter the hallway carrying a fresh cup of coffee.

"Tired, my daughter?" she asked as she gently brushed back Morgana's hair. "

"A little. There's no change in Father's condition."

"Go rest now. I'll take over." Marisol handed her the motel key.

"Mother?" Morgana studied her mother's face. "You're smiling. Looks like you're really rested. Your face has a ... radiance ... a glow like a warm moon. How do you feel?"

Marisol kissed her daughter on her forehead. "I had a dream—of Isadora. She told me your father would be fine. In time, he would heal and in the dream I was happy again—as happy as I was as a young child." She released Morgana and stood staring lovingly at her daughter's long, satin-textured hair, at her deep hazel eyes, her olive skin and her fine dark brows, implanting them forever in her memory. "I love you. Without you, my life would have been so empty, so useless, for you are my only child." She gently kissed Morgana's cheek.

Morgana drew away from Marisol, remembering the conversation she had heard in the barn between Eagle Eyes and Tom. "Mother, do you regret not having another child?"

"Yes. But the look in your father's eyes when you came into this world more than compensated for not having another child! You pleased him so much. It was magic, the love that passed between you and your father. How his chest swelled with pride, and how the tears fell from his eyes. Yes, my princess, the three year wait was worth every sacrifice. You pleased us both." Marisol was surprised to see her daughter's eyes suddenly filled with tears.

"Mother, you mean you were married for three years before my conception?"

"Yes, it was that way—as Isadora said it would be."

Morgana breathed deeply before she asked, "Mother, was Father your first great love?"

A far-away haze masked Marisol's face. "No. There was a man. A man destined to be chief, whom I loved greatly, but that love was not favored. He was Bold Feather, father of Eagle Eyes."

"You mean I am not half sister to Eagle Eyes!"

Marisol gasped, "Of course not! Where did your get such a crazy idea?" she turned away, stunned.

"Oh, Mother, it was just something I misunderstood." She gently placed her hand on Marisol's arms, seeking to close the distance between them and erase the frown that now masked Marisol's face. "Mother, please. It was a foolish question."

Marisol nodded, "Yes, it was. Now go, daughter, get some rest, for such questions must mean you are extremely tired." She picked up Morgana's bag and handed it to her.

"Mother, I'm concerned about you right now. Just look at your face—it's as though you've seen the source of life, our Great Spirit. Your face is so peaceful and serene, it's almost a blessing, and the light that sparkles in your eyes is like none that I've seen. Morgana reached up to touch her mother's face.

Marisol laughed softly. "I dreamt of Isadora. She set my path right. She lifted the fog that surrounded me and it was as if all my faith in mankind and the spirit world was restored. In the dream, Isadora reminded me that our destiny is a set plan and each plan is given according to the spirit of a person. In my old age I have forgotten much. In the dream, I was exploring an unknown mountain while Isadora was explaining all life's secrets to me." She smiled upon seeing a confused look cross Morgana's face. "Just remember that you are both Navajo and Mexican; you have a dual heritage. Follow the path of your destiny with your chin unquivering and your head held high, no matter where it leads you."

"Mother! I'm a person that has a foot in two different cultures and I'm not totally accepted by either race."

Marisol quickly interrupted her. "That is the old Indian way. Times are changing and you belong to a new generation of young people. You are Navajo and Mexican—both proud races. You have done a fine job of blending in with each. We are brother races, as close as the eagle and the hawk, as close as the coyote and the wolf. We are alike, both survivors. Remember, I love you just as you are, Navajo and Mexican. Above all, you are mine and his." She turned her gaze to her husband. A slight shudder overcame her, then she sighed as if she were ready to fight a fierce battle.

Morgana kissed Marisol's cheek. She then said goodnight and walked down the corridor, glancing back to see her mother enter her father's room. Her mother had lost weight. Even her skirt was hanging loosely. Morgana watched her mother from the hallway, then slowly turned to leave the hospital. Tomorrow morning, she would speak to her about going to the ranch for a short rest. Cousin Tom would gladly drive her back home. The time away would do her good.

As Morgana walked slowly toward the motel, she inhaled the crisp night air, which gently awakened her. The deep blue hue of the sky was streaked with the glorious pink rays of sunset. Such brilliant colors, she mused, silently worshiping the Great Spirit that created the heavens for people like her to gaze upon. Soon the bewitching Moon would send its rays like silver spears to light the darkness that would envelop the world in harmonious colors. This blending of the colors of Mother Earth, Father Sky and mankind was indeed a marvelous thing.

Isadora had told her long ago that, for the Navajo, everything is religious. Everything the Navajo knows, such as his hogan, his fields, his livestock, the heavens above and the dirt upon which he walks is considered holy. Thinking about her mother's beliefs, Morgana decided that she needed to be more aware of the world about her; and she resolved to enjoy the small things in life. Things that she had been ignoring daily. Simple things like a misplaced wildflower.

She crossed the street to the motel. Then, as she put the key in the lock and opened the door, she found herself face to face with Eagle Eyes. "Morgana, we must talk," he said immediately.

Eagle Eyes shut the door behind her. She is beautiful, he thought. And, like most beautiful things, she is costly. He glanced longingly down at her, then leaned against the door and studied her. No words transpired between them. Will it always be thus, he wondered? He wanted to talk but just as he was about to speak, the loud ring of the phone startled them. He reached out to pick up the receiver before she could move.

"Yes!" he spoke sharply, angry at being interrupted. "What? This can't be!" He glanced at Morgana, hesitating. He slowly handed her the receiver. "Morgana," he said softly as he gently looked into her face, "it's the hospital."

She quickly put the receiver to her ear. "Yes, Dr. Alonzo, this is Morgana Cruz." A moment of silence transpired and then a low moan escaped her lips as the receiver fell from her hand. She screamed a loud, sad wail that filled the room with the dark vibrations that only the news of a death can create.

Eagle Eyes took her in his arms, held her, then spoke into the phone. "We'll be there shortly." He replaced the receiver on its hook, then looked down at her. "There's nothing we can do. Your mother has crossed! The transition has started." He let her cry on his shoulder, not forcing her to do a thing and not wanting to do a thing himself. Eagle Eyes sensed only that he was suddenly very weary. Perhaps, he thought, my tribal burden is too great. Must I be always the one who bids a last farewell to my people?

Morgana's sobs were so heart-rending that her whole body shook. No, she thought, Mother could not be gone—it was a mistake! Father is the one who is ill. "No! No!" she cried over and over again, not feeling the black leather of Eagle Eyes' jacket pressed tightly against her face.

A cold wind seeped into the room. Where had it come from? "Mother!" she screamed. "Mother, I need you!" she cried, unaware that Eagle Eyes had escaped into a trance. The light around them had diminished into a cold, eerie darkness.

Chapter 12

Once again Morgana stood facing Eagle Eyes in the high sierras. Her mother's body, wrapped in a white bear skin rug, lay on a platform between them. Morgana was pale and trimmer than she'd ever been. The cold wind slapped her face, but she showed no pain. She vaguely remembered Dr. Alonzo speaking to her, but she did not recall accepting the official death certificate.

Her eyes, saddened by death, looked to Eagle Eyes who seemed distant— as if he too had lost a great battle. Now his fierce eyes were softer when he looked upon her. The defiance and anger were dashed out of them and replaced by a reckoning with death and the cold weather. He who knew all suddenly seemed at a loss about many things. She remembered him at the hospital talking to the doctor, then to Cousin Tom, and finally turning to her, demanding an immediate answer.

"Will your mother be buried the Indian way or not?" He had taken her by the shoulders and shaken the answer out of her. Didn't he realize how much his hands pinched her shoulders? "Decide now! The decision is yours!" he stated, with no regard for her feelings of loss and helplessness. And, when she was unable to provide an immediate answer, he added coldly, "Your father cannot help you—he is close to death himself. You alone must decide. Everyone waits for your answer. If you wait much longer the hospital people will call the funeral home to pick her body up and then it will be too late! Decide!"

Morgana flinched upon hearing his words. "The Indian way," she muttered. "She is Indian." She cried, as Cousin Tom held her in his arms and comforted her.

"You decided right, my cousin. She would be proud," Cousin Tom had whispered in her ear as he held her tightly. But Morgana pried herself away and fled into the ICU room to be with her father. Ever so gently she knelt beside him and softly cried into the fold of his arm. "Oh, Father. Please don't leave me too."

Much later Tom Crooked Leg tiptoed into the room. He lifted Morgana from her knees and sat her in a chair. He placed her hands around a cup of hot coffee and stood studying the man his cousin had married years ago. Yes, he thought, they must have been happy in their own way.

Tom Crooked Leg glanced at Morgana. The sedative should work fairly fast, especially since he'd dissolved it into the steaming liquid. Then, when she was fast asleep, he would drive her back to the ranch for a rest before the burial ceremonies. The following day Eagle Eyes could take her for the purification ceremonies. Since Marisol had no property to burn and had married out of the tribe, the ceremonies would be easier and more convenient. She would be taken to her burial spot in full ceremonial attire.

Now, on Marisol's burial day, Eagle Eyes glanced up to meet Morgana's tear-stained gaze. His heart ached to see her so desolate and lost. Because of the extremely cold weather, a group of men had been allowed into the sacred grounds to build Marisol's platform in advance. They had come willingly, but he still paid them handsomely for their services, forcing them to take the money not for themselves, but for their families.

Now that the prayers and the chants were completed, he stood tall and proud before her, but with a much faltering spirit. What should she do now? He held out his hand to her, welcoming her to his warmth and protection, but she did not move. She stood as if frozen in place, unseeing, unfeeling.

After a few moments, he said softly, "It is over. Come." And he left her standing there with the snowflakes drifting past her. The white delicate snowflakes blessed her bowed head and lay softly upon her shiny, black hair. She cried, wanting the darkness that pierced her heart to go away, but it would not.

"Isadora!" she prayed, "please meet Mama's spirit. Keep her unafraid as she travels through the new world." She fell to her knees, sobbing. "Mother!"

Eagle Eyes heard her sad wail as it echoed over the mountain tops, but forced himself to walk on toward the lodge where he would build a fire, then return to get her. By then she should have given in to her grief and be easier to handle. He would prepare a special tea to make her rest.

The burial lodge was warm and the animal skins placed on the outside walls kept the increasing cold from penetrating its warm cocoon. It was time to fetch Morgana. In minutes it would be dark and the snow would get deeper. They should leave by morning lest they get stranded. Eagle Eyes had thrown some extra blankets on the horses and tied them securely in a small opening among some large boulders. He knew they would be fine; however, he would check them once more before walking the trail to get Morgana.

The animals sensed his presence as he held out some carrots for them. The warrior horse seemed greatly pleased to be alongside the quick pinto La Luna. Eagle Eyes spoke to each of them as if they were great chiefs to be reckoned with fairly, and they understood that it was a sorrowful time which demanded much patience on their part. He kissed each horse on the forehead directly behind the eyes, then turned a worried glance up the path.

If only Morgana were as easy to handle as the horses. He understood most women, but she was different—she made simple things difficult. He needed to be much kinder to her, he decided, as he trudged up the path. After all, she'd lost so much in such a short time! But her attitude unnerved him. He would not expect much from her, but kindness would be his gift to her from now on.

His observing eyes quickly spotted Morgana as she made her way down the mountain, her frail body covered with snow. He rushed to assist her when he saw her fall into the deep snowdrifts and tumble a few feet down the mountain. He reached her and swept her up in his arms, then hurried back to the lodge, cursing himself for being such a hard-hearted person. She was not in her right mind and he should have watched over her more carefully.

Morgana gently laid her head upon his shoulder, not caring whether or not he left her buried in the snow.

A sad memory suddenly came to Eagle Eyes. He remembered his old aunt who had carried him like this when, as a young boy, he had tried to kill himself by jumping off a high cliff. He stepped carefully to avoid slipping on an ice-covered rock. The darkness encircled them as he hurried the last few yards to the warmth of the lodge.

He placed Morgana on a blanket, then quickly pulled a bear skin over her. He threw two pieces of wood into the fire, then crawled under his own bearskin.

He watched Morgana as her eyes closed slowly from exhaustion. He listened to the howling wind outside, to an occasional hoof beating upon the ground, and to the hiss and crackle of the fire. A look of peace and contentment beamed from his face as he fell into a light sleep, dreaming of all those whom he had laid to rest up above the mountain top. His soul gaily greeted those spirits of yesterday and suddenly the spirit of Isadora placed herself between him and Morgana and sang to them. "It is as it should be," she said just before she disappeared.

♡   ♡   ♡

Eagle Eyes woke up instantly, listening to the wind which howled much like a crazed coyote. Isadora had taught him that coyotes were filled with evil powers that enabled them to interfere with people's affairs and that they could turn up anywhere and at anytime. Now, coyote was near. There was no noise from the horses, but he reached for his rifle and threw another log on the fire which burned low; still, he listened.

Morgana turned her head restlessly. She receded into her dreams once again, dreaming of Marisol, who was humming softly to herself as she picked wild flowers in an open meadow. How young she looked, Morgana realized, even in her dream, for Marisol looked exactly like the girl in the tapestry.

♡   ♡   ♡

When daybreak arrived, Eagle Eyes rose and left the lodge. The snow was deeper than he'd imagined. They must get down the mountain now or else face a greater threat. The horses were chewing on some hay that he'd left for them. He hurriedly saddled them and then re-entered the lodge.

Morgana was sitting up. Her hair was in disarray and she felt drained of all energy.

He warmed his hands near the fire, then handed her a biscuit from a basket nearby. She refused it by simply turning away. "We must leave today ... within the hour. It will be worse tonight," Eagle Eye said as he bit into the biscuit and chewed slowly, watching her face.

She sat silently staring into the fire as he went about making a hot tea for her to drink. "Drink this; it will be cold as we go down the mountain." He saw defiance streak across her eyes, so he quickly added, "You can return in the spring. I shall guide you up." He covered her shoulders with a blanket, then added, "Your mother's passage is complete. It is your father who needs you now."

Yes, Father, thought Morgana as she sipped the hot tea. I must help him. Her eyes followed every move that Eagle Eyes made as he quickly and expertly packed their belongings. When she finished, he held out his hand to her to help her to her feet and wrapped her coat tightly about her. Outside the lodge he asked, "Do you need to relieve yourself?" He turned to tie the packs on the horses and dared not watch her follow a small path to a low clump of trees.

When she returned, he helped her mount La Luna, then secured the blankets around her. "We shall not be stopping until we are down the mountain." He mounted, then gave the lead to his warrior horse as he searched the sky for the sun. We shall be frozen by the time we arrive, he thought. It was lucky he told Tom Crooked Leg to be on the look-out for flares, in case there should be trouble. He did not notice Morgana turn to stare up to the top of the sacred mountain where her mother now rested.

Mother, her soul screamed. How can I leave you? The wind whistled, creating a snowfilled whirlwind around her.

By late that afternoon, Morgana no longer felt her body. The cold had numbed her so that an occasional blink of her eyes was all she could manage.

If she'd had a voice, she would have called for Eagle Eyes to stop and build a fire, but she could not manage even that much.

The flare that Eagle Eyes shot up suddenly startled her. She shook so that chunks of snow slid off her blankets much like lava falling off a spurting hot volcano. Minutes later, the sound of a motor echoed through the snow covered valley. Tom Crooked Leg's jeep stopped at the base of the mountain.

"Hello!" cried Eagle Eyes, waving frantically.

"Welcome, friends!" yelled Tom Crooked Leg as he ran to help Eagle Eyes dismount and quickly brushed off the snow from the horses' blankets while Eagle Eyes pulled Morgana down from her horse and carried her to the warm jeep. He gently placed her on the seat, then covered her with dry, warm blankets. His hand gently brushed her ice-cold cheek. She glanced up as he slammed the door shut.

He is so strong, she thought, watching him help Tom Crooked Leg with the horses. He should be tired by now yet he never rests. He continues onward and it seems as though he never looks back, never re-examines his past actions. Is he afraid to remember, she wondered?

Tom Crooked Leg slid into the driver seat as Eagle Eyes crawled into the back seat. They drove in silence, the small caravan moving slowly toward the Palo Verde Ranch belonging to Eagle Eyes.

Morgana's body was tingling as it thawed out, and at first, she took no notice of their route. It was close to an hour before she noticed that she was not familiar with this northern territory. She turned to Eagle Eyes but, except for an occasional glance back to see if Tom was okay, he did nothing special to indicate he was lost.

"Where are we going?" she asked in almost a whisper, noting that her lips felt blistered and cracked.

"To my place. There we will rest and recover," he added, not turning to face her.

"Couldn't we make it to the hospital?" she asked, covering her sore lips with the edge of the blanket hoping the warmth would aid them.

"No, it is too far."

She wanted to argue, but resisted, knowing it would be of no use. Her toes itched and stung as they thawed. She wished she could stick her hands and feet in hot steaming water to help the thawing process. How she would like to forget this last month entirely. It had been a trying, exhausting time and as with this first snow storm, there was more to come. She was anxious to see her father. There were things to tend to at the ranch. Suddenly she started to giggle as she thought of her wedding vase. She resolved that, as soon as she got home, she would throw it against the boulder at the base of her mountain and watch it shatter into a million pieces.

Eagle Eyes watched her curiously from the corner of his eyes. This is not going well, he thought. Her mind still wanders.

The road north consisted of mountains and valleys one after another. For a while they followed the Río Grande River, but then they split from it and followed a dirt road up towards a mountain. They passed under a tangled umbrella of pinon trees, then came to a clearing at the base of a boulder-covered mountain. There, centered in a small clearing, was a log home of two stories with snow caked upon its roof and smoke bellowing out of a chimney. It looked inviting and warm, a place for a hidden retreat, Morgana thought.

Eagle Eyes stopped the truck and waved at Tom Crooked Leg to continue toward the barn. Then he opened the door to allow Morgana out, catching her as her feet hit the ground. She flinched, not expecting the pain in her legs, and he immediately supported her against his chest, gazing for a moment into her troubled hazel eyes.

"I'll carry you inside." He swung her up in his arms, hurried to the front door, which was not locked, and entered a spacious entry way. He slowly let her down. "Welcome to my home," he added shyly.

"Winter Star!" he yelled loudly as he led Morgana into the sparsely furnished living room.

An old woman who quickly dried her hands upon her apron hurried out of the hallway. "Oh, Rusty. Welcome!" She gave him a tight hug.

"Winter Star. This is Morgana. Make her welcome. She can use the bedroom upstairs. Draw a hot bath for her." He turned and smiled at Morgana, enjoying the surprised look upon her face, then he quickly left through the front door, heading to the barn.

"Please come." Winter Star motioned for Morgana to follow her. "He did not tell me you were coming."

Morgana followed the silver-haired woman as she shuttled down a long hallway, then up the stairs, talking more to herself than to Morgana. "He is a good boy, my Rusty." She held open a door leading to a bedroom with walls of light pine.

The bed was covered with a handmade quilt of bold colored stars, but it was the tapestry on the wall that brought tears to Morgana's eyes, for she immediately recognized it as one of Marisol's early accomplishments. The tapestry bore the Mourning Doves, who, like the roadrunner and the turkey, are idealized by the Navajo. Mourning Dove reported things reliably and did not have an equal in speed. Mourning Dove understood special Navajo war language and, thereby, caused his people to win battles. Morgana smiled, remembering how Marisol jerked her head back and forth to imitate the Dove. She'd forgotten about the story, for she had been around ten when

Marisol had told it to her as she wove the tapestry. To find it here seemed unbelievable. She reached out to it seeking her mother's soothing touch.

"You like it, no?" Winter Star emerged from the adjoining bath. "Indian princess made it many moons ago. A great princess, the last, they say. I never see her." She smiled a toothless grin, then patted Morgana on the shoulder. "You bathe, I go fix bath for Rusty, then we eat." She reached out and took a fistful of Morgana's hair. "Good hair. You wash. I dry for you, okay?" She smiled, then left Morgana alone.

The bathroom was large and the tub, filled with hot steaming water, was inviting. She found a robe hanging behind the linen door. The hot water felt comforting to her; yet, it could not stop her tears.

♡   ♡   ♡

Tom Crooked Leg unsaddled La Luna. "Fine *señorita!*" he whispered softly into the pinto's ear. You're a real beauty."

Eagle Eyes turned, "Tom, if you could talk to women like you talk to horses, you'd have a fine wife by now."

Tom hung up La Luna's bridle. "No woman wants a one-legged man, especially one like me." He laughed.

"There's plenty of women around who would accept less," argued Eagle Eyes.

"Not for me, Eagle Eyes. But, for you my friend, women would kill!"

Eagle Eyes laughed. "Killing is no easy matter regardless of which law we abide by."

"That is true, my brother. If you don't mind, I shall ask Winter Star for something to eat, then I shall be off. That stallion, Santos, is a stubborn horse and he may break loose if he is not fed. Old man Cruz has him well-schooled to obey only him, so he is not adjusting well."

Eagle Eyes asked, "Please check the house as well. Make sure everything is in order. We'll meet at the Cruz ranch in the morning."

"Yes, I will do that too," Tom Crooked Legs added. They talked in hushed tones and slowly walked toward the house.

Winter Star greeted them at the back door with an amused twinkle in her eye. These two men were her favorites. "Ah, boys, come. Clean up! Supper is ready!" She took their coats and hung them up. "Wash now," she added.

Tom quickly took the old woman in his arms. "Winter Star, the heavens will fall because I cannot stay for supper. But, the Great Spirit shall be pleased if you packed a bite or two to take with me. There are other matters to which I must attend." He gave her a quick kiss, which Winter Star playfully ducked.

"Ah, so, it shall be only two for supper. A real beauty this one is too." She glanced at Eagle Eyes who was on his way out of the kitchen.

"Oh, Winter Star, you speak of my beautiful little cousin. Yes, she is a beauty, but her eyes do not shine for your boy here. He must work harder to impress this princess." Tom laughed merrily when he saw the old woman's face fall.

Not true, she thought. All women love Rusty. They cannot help themselves for "he who knows all" is overpowering. She wanted more information. "Cousin, you say?"

"Yes, my cousin she is," Tom replied. "Now, how about a plate of food that I can eat while you make my lunch to take on the road. I am terribly hungry."

"Yes, my boy. Sit, sit!"

♡   ♡   ♡

After Tom Crooked Leg had left, Winter Star quickly set a simple but pretty table for Rusty and his guest. Their meal consisted of baked chicken, baked potatoes and fresh broccoli. Earlier in the day, she had baked his favorite dessert—apple pie.

Winter Star had lived with Rusty since Isadora had found her in a desolate state and had brought her to care for the boy soon after the death of his aunt. She lived with Rusty as his housekeeper, his cook and his home guardian and had taken an immediate liking to the lonely boy. They had grown together, both older and wiser. He was all she had, especially since Isadora's passing, and she loved tending to his needs. She was old now, nearly seventy five, and it was time for Rusty to find a decent wife and settle down.

This girl was the first he'd ever brought here. She was aware that he frequented the reservation hut quite often and that there was another woman who had never been to his new home. A gleam of pleasure ignited in her eye. Perhaps this young woman was special. She quickly pulled out two candle sticks and arranged them in the center of the table, then she hurried to the fireplace to rekindle it. Tonight, she decided, must be exceptional. She shuffled down the hallway and up the stairs to do the girl's hair.

"May I enter, my girl?" she asked, knocking softly on the door.

"Yes," answered Morgana as she got up from resting on the bed.

Winter Star immediately noticed the redness around her eyes. Something was wrong. There should be no tears tonight. "Come, sit here while I do your hair." She motioned to a chair that rested in front of a simple desk. Then she brought a towel and a brush and comb from the bathroom. The towel she expertly draped around Morgana's shoulders. "Good hair," she said as she began to comb it. "Would you like braids pulled back from the sides and fastened in the back?"

"Anything will do," answered Morgana, not caring to speak. Her eyes kept glancing up at the tapestry that hung on the wall.

Winter Star combed Morgana's hair, all the time thinking that the girl's soul was hurting. When she'd finished, the girl would look simple but lovely enough to entice Rusty, she thought. Her old fingers worked fast to braid each section. She tied the two braids with a tiny yellow ribbon. "There. Now I must find you something to wear."

Morgana shrugged. "I have nothing."

Winter Star smiled. "But, I have something that Rusty brought me long ago. Wait, I shall return!" She hurried down the stairs and out of the house to her cabin.

From the upstairs window, Morgana saw the old woman rush past the yard below. What is she doing? she wondered. In minutes Winter Star shuffled back to the house and into the room.

She carried a box which she placed on the bed, then immediately opened it. "See!" From the box she pulled out an embroidered Mexican dress. It was black with many colorful roses all over it. True, Winter Star thought, it is for summer wear, but I will throw another log onto the fire to keep the living room warm and cozy.

Morgana reached out to touch the dress. "It is nice. I am honored to wear it." She removed her robe and slipped on the dress, then she stood facing Winter Star who nodded her approval.

"Oh, wait!" Once again the old woman shuffled down the stairs to a hall closet. Morgana heard her grumbling, but she returned with a pair of crocheted black slippers. "Now you are ready." She took Morgana's hand and led her to the kitchen where she opened a drawer and pulled out a stick of cinnamon which she rolled across Morgana's wrists. "A poor woman's perfume." She giggled happily as she watched Morgana's eyes widen with wonder.

Morgana could not resist smiling. Then Winter Star held the stick out to roll across her neck. Morgana laughed. "I would never have thought of that."

No, thought Winter Star, but he loves the scent of cinnamon and if in my pies, why not on you? She winked happily at Morgana. "Tonight is a quite special time." She added gaily, then turned sharply when Eagle Eyes entered the kitchen.

"I'm starving, Winter Star. Is supper ready?" he added, moving to the stove and lifting the lid off a pan.

Morgana lowered her lashes, but not before noticing how clean cut and fresh he looked. He'd shaved and his hair was neatly pulled back in a tight clasp at the back. A single piece of leather was wrapped several times around his hair, then tied in a neat knot. With her eyes still lowered she noticed his clean well-pressed jeans, his neatly shined boots, and his black western shirt open at the throat.

"Yes, yes, supper is ready. Go out. I serve." She motioned for Morgana to move toward the door, then anxiously flushed Eagle Eyes out of her kitchen and into the dining room.

Morgana entered the dining room and stood behind a chair nervously waiting for him. When he entered, she quickly said, "I am not hungry."

He pulled out her chair. "Winter Star will be disappointed if you do not eat the food she has especially prepared for us." He added, "Please, she is old. Humor her." He said it softly, indicating for her to sit.

"Yes, I would not want to disappoint her. She is so nice and concerned." Morgana seated herself.

"It's good to be home," he added as he walked around the table to hand her some mint tea.

Sadly she bowed her head, longing for her home, her own room and her parents.

"Sorry." He gently touched her shoulder. "It's just that I really enjoy being home. I mean here, this is home for me, not particularly the cabin on the reservation. Tribal business is conducted out of the hut there." He seated himself across from Morgana and smiled, lowering his head as he tried to hide a smile.

"What is it?" she asked, wondering what his smile meant.

"It's just that ... .well, I'm used to seeing Winter Star sitting there hanging onto my every word."

She immediately rose. "I'll move."

"No!" he snapped. "No," he added softly, "I want you to sit there. She ... you ... well, it's that the house has never been visited by a female guest." He quickly lifted his glass to toast her. "Welcome, Morgana Cruz, to my home."

She smiled. "Thank you." Then she took a slow sip from her glass but kept her eyes lowered at the plate before her, glancing up only when Winter Star entered with a platter of chicken and a bowl of steaming broccoli.

Winter Star placed the food near Eagle Eyes, glanced with approval at Morgana, then retreated to get the rest of the food. Winter Star quickly returned with the rolls and added, "Now I have something to do in my little hut. Carlo awaits me. Leave everything and I will clean it up in the morning." She smiled encouragingly at Morgana, then left the room.

Morgana heard the back door slam shut. "Who is Carlo?"

"Please pass me your plate and I'll serve you." He deliberately took his time in filling her plate before he added, "Carlo is her cat." He smiled.

"Oh," she said as she reached out to take the plate he handed her. Morgana took small bites of her food, forcing it down, all the while wishing it were not so quiet. Her mind played touch and go with her, as moments of sadness suddenly came to her, then quickly disappeared. He paid no particular attention to her, but she could see that he was very hungry. He was polite and neat, but his hunger prevented him from talking. For this she was thankful. The click and clatter of the utensils were the only sounds she heard until he'd finished.

Then he watched her take an occasional bite of food. She eats like a sparrow, he thought, before deciding to take seconds himself. He offered her more, but she refused. Then he glanced over at the freshly cut apple pie and decided to wait until later to serve it. "If you're finished, you may sit by the fire." He motioned toward the fireplace, then rose and pulled out her chair.

In the living room the only place to sit was on a sofa. He went around and sat within an arm's reach from her and stared into the blazing fire, silently allowing his mind to drift away.

Morgana trembled. No. She willed her body to be still. I will not cry. I will not break down. I am in control, she told herself repeatedly. It is not as if he were a stranger. We've eaten together, we've argued and buried our dead together. He's been there when I've needed him and, yes, he is terrifying and challenging, so unlike Father. No, she changed her mind. He is very much like Father. She glanced over at him, but he was watching her and she trembled more. "When can I go home?" she asked in a whisper.

He did not answer, but rose quickly and opened a nearby oak chest from which he pulled out a small lap blanket. For a brief moment he stood directly behind her and then gently placed the blanket over her shoulders. He then looked down at her before he bent down to whisper in her ear. "We've been through much together. At least allow me to be your friend."

He slowly inhaled the fragrance of her hair but quickly let go of her shoulders, afraid that being so close to her would drive him into turmoil. She was frightened enough. "Home, you say? Early in the morning I shall take you home."

He walked over to the large window and looked out into the cold, blue darkness. He pressed his hand against the cold panes in hopes of cooling them. It's incredible, he thought. Why, of all the women he knew, should he be entangled with one who did not desire him, one who was only half-clan? She could slowly drive him out of his mind and her slow, charming smile could change all that he believed in, all that he had achieved in this last decade. He placed his forehead against the cool glass and closed his eyes. Perhaps, he thought, it's best to go to bed. He was really tired.

He decided to bid her good-night. When he turned back, he noticed she had moved to stand before the fireplace. The blanket was now wrapped tightly around her shoulders as she stood staring into the flaming blaze. Her luscious, gleaming hair sent sparks flying into the air and as her tear-filled eyes rose to meet his, his heart increased its rhythm. She is so beautiful, he thought silently.

"What is it?" he asked. "Have I hurt you?"

Slowly, she turned to him. "It's been so hard," she began. "I wish there had been more time for me and my mother. Now, I wonder if there will be time left for me and my father. And ... what if there were no tomorrow for me ... or even for you?"

He hesitated and slowly wiped his forehead with his hand. "I never know of tomorrow. I see too many ends and never enough tomorrows. It is what I do. It is my duty and responsibility with the tribe to make a decent ending for those now departed." No longer wishing to discuss death, he moved toward the door leading down the hallway to his bedroom.

"Then do not leave yet," she added, "for who knows what tomorrow brings."

He turned back quickly and stood for a moment analyzing the meaning of her words, "Do not play games with me, Morgana Cruz. I am a tired man," he said.

"I know, but I do not play games and I too am tired. Let's sit in peace. Let us help each other erase our sorrows."

"So be it," he whispered as he moved to the couch, sat down, then drew her to him.

Morgana rested her head on his shoulder and quietly sobbed as he stared solemnly into the blazing fire. After a while he gently kissed her forehead. "If I could change things, I would ... you know."

She answered in a whisper as she wiped away her tears. "My life has broken into a thousand pieces. My heart has broken and continues to break. I do not understand all these changes."

"I know," he said as he pulled her closer. "I feel that same way when I heal someone who wishes to live no longer." They both stared into the bright fire which temporarily soothed them. "Morgana Cruz, what shall I do with you?" he whispered softly.

Chapter 13

Eagle Eyes woke early the next morning feeling refreshed and happier than he'd ever been in a long time. He peeked into the guest bedroom and noticed that Morgana had not stirred. Let her rest, he thought. I'll send Winter Star to help her later. Right now, there were things to do. He needed to check on Mr. Cruz's condition and to touch base with Tom at the Cruz place.

Winter Star had cleaned up the kitchen, Eagle Eyes noted, realizing he could not imagine living without her. He dialed the hospital and waited to be switched to the ICU ward. The nurse told him that Mr. Cruz was breathing better and had been taken off the respirator, but he was still not conscious and would remain in the ward until the following day. He thanked the nurse, then hung up as Winter Star entered the kitchen.

A merry twinkle gleamed from the eye of Winter Star. "It is as it should be!" she said happily, nudging him playfully.

He smiled at her, then added, "So it is!" He hugged her. "Now, go help her. We have a full day ahead of us."

The old woman shuffled out of the kitchen while he went outside to load the horses onto the trailer.

Winter Star looked down upon Morgana. She wished the young woman could stay for another day. The time with Rusty would do them both good. But, Rusty was not one for staying put. Others demanded too much for him. Winter Star hated to wake her, but Rusty was anxious and there was breakfast to fix for them before they left. "Hey, girl!" Winter Star called, stooping as far as she could in order to scrutinize Morgana. "Wake up!"

Morgana woke with a start, then settled back in bed when she saw Winter Star.

"You rested? Yes?" smiled Winter Star. "Come, he waits." She laughed and left the room.

Morgana rose and decided to take the opportunity to explore Eagle Eyes's room, which was at the foot of the stairs. She found the room was large but as sparse as a monk's cell. He who knows all has no need for frivolous items, she thought. Aside from the large double bed, the room contained a bookshelf filled with books and a desk near his bed. His bathroom held only the necessities and some extra towels. Her father, she remembered, had many bottles of cologne, but Eagle Eyes had books even in his bathroom. She smiled. Eagle Eyes simplified his surroundings and she found she liked that.

The house smelled of fresh cedar logs. Morgana thought it was no more than three or four years old. The uncluttered spaciousness along with its few antiques made it ideal. She sensed that the favorite room was the large kitchen where Eagle Eyes and Winter Star seemed most content. Unlike the kitchen at her home which was on the lower level and used only when necessary, Winter Star's kitchen was a meeting place to discuss the trials or happy moments of the day.

Eagle Eyes and Winter Star were sitting together at the large table in the center of the kitchen when she entered. Neither rose to greet her, but both pointed at a chair at their side.

"Greetings, Winter Star," Morgana said, then turned to Eagle Eyes. "Shall I call you Eagle Eyes or Rusty?" she questioned as she took the plate that Winter Star offered her.

"Call me what you like," he said.

"Then, it shall be Eagle Eyes, for he is the person I know best."

Winter Star rose and shuffled to the stove. Eagle Eyes took the opportunity to whisper, "Do you feel well?"

"I'm better," she said softly, feeling herself blush.

He smiled his approval, then filled her glass with juice. "Eat, for we have much to do today."

"Really? I'd like to see my father."

"Later. I promise." He noticed her slightly raised eyebrows, then quickly added, "I've called the hospital. He's better. But, with my herbs, he'll progress rapidly."

Morgana argued, "I should be there!"

"I understand, but we must take La Luna to the ranch and tend to the other stock first. Okay?"

"But, my father needs me more than ever!" she replied.

"Right. And I promise I'll take you there as soon as everything is settled at your place." He shook his head, not wanting to upset her further. "Eat now. Even our beasts must eat on cold days," he reminded her.

After a quick breakfast, Morgana hugged Winter Star good-bye and promised to come visit again. Eagle Eyes waited impatiently by the truck. Then Morgana joined him, glancing in the trailer to check on La Luna.

"She's fine," added Eagle Eyes. "So is Warrior Horse."

"Good. La Luna is precious to me."

"And, perhaps, I'm not?" he said gazing down into her eyes.

Not knowing what to answer, she purposely turned her attention to La Luna.

"I understand," he said as he walked to the cab of the truck. To his surprise, she had upset him.

♡   ♡   ♡

They drove into the main entrance of the Cruz ranch, and Morgana immediately noticed that the house looked cold and deserted. She never took her eyes off the beloved stone structure. "It'll never be the same without Mother." Her heart swelled and the lump in her throat would not dissolve.

Eagle Eyes reached over and took her hand encouragingly, squeezing it. "Change is hard. The strong move forward and the weak fall into the dark depths of gloom. Think about tomorrow and the help you will be to your father. This will be hard for him as well. Time will pass and your soul shall heal."

Words would not come to her. She only nodded that she understood.

They saw Tom Crooked Leg hobbling out of the barn. "Hello! Was the drive an easy one?"

Eagle Eyes opened the door of the truck and greeted him with a tight bear hug.

"Little cousin, how are you?" Tom asked as he hugged Morgana.

"Okay," she answered, brushing flakes of new fallen snow from her eyelashes and then gazing toward the house.

Tom noticed her glance and immediately asked, "Would little cousin like to go inside? I have started a fire and there is hot coffee. He took her gently by the elbow and turned to lead her up the path.

She hesitated. "Thanks, Tom. I want to go up there alone." She searched his face for understanding. The two men stood in the snow watching her as she walked slowly up the path.

Morgana carefully turned the handle of the old Spanish doors. She hesitated a moment, then carefully and sadly laid her head against the antique panel, sensing an enormous emptiness overtake her. No one waited to greet her. No longer would Marisol drop whatever she was doing to sit and talk with her. Her father would not invite her to join him at the fireplace. It would all be different now.

She twisted the door knob and entered. In the foyer, she stood staring at the staircase, listening to the empty house. The sound of her boots upon the Spanish tiles echoed as she walked toward the large den, sensing that the blazing fire Tom had started had already warmed the room. Standing behind the William and Mary chair, she gently ran her hand over its velvet back, seeking the answer to all that had happened recently. As she stared up at the tapestry, tears filled her eyes. Mother, she thought, as she wiped her eyes, how I wish you were here. She sniffled and helplessly stared at her surroundings as memories sprang in her mind, haunting her like dark shadows that penetrate nightmares. Beside her lay her father's favorite pipe. She picked it up and examined it.

What shall I do now, she questioned? Just this morning she'd felt full of new-found energy. Now, she was totally depleted. She rose, ran up the stairs to her room. As she passed her parents' room she hesitated, then pushed open the door. A room once bright and busy now lay in a dark gloom. Her mother's things. What would she do with them? She ran from the room, slammed the door shut and ran up the stairs to the safety of her room.

A while later, Eagle Eyes searched the den for Morgana. Not finding her there, he opened the door to the library and stood speechless at the great number of books. Some were rare books and others were the latest best sellers. The center of the room was graced by an enormous carved desk and two well-used leather chairs with a marble-topped table between them. A pipe lay on the table. The room was cluttered and used. Obviously Mr. Cruz's favorite place, he deduced, because of the masculine feeling in the room. Yes, he thought, as he stepped back and took in the surroundings, I would like this room too, especially the astonishing stained glass that graced the large high windows which let in just the proper amount of light.

As he walked through the rooms of the house, he saw that it had a certain old world charm. It would sell quickly for a good price, especially since the materials were of the finest quality, like the Spanish floral tiles which covered the floor of the foyer and the upstairs hallway. Yes, he could see some rich European or, perhaps, a movie star eagerly buying the ranch to use as a desert treasure to show off in the bright sunlit skies of New Mexico. That is, if the old man died.

"Morgana!" he called as he stepped through the door of the master bedroom and peered into the semi-darkened room. Her parents' room, he realized, as he suddenly spied the small connecting door. "Morgana!" He walked over to the small door and slowly pushed it open.

Marisol's workroom was as sparsely furnished as was his own. A well-organized shelf, the size of the entire length of the room, contained various hues of threads, yarns and tools. The loom seemed incredibly large in the room, almost monopolizing it. In the opposite corner hung an old "*Yei*" blanket. Eagle Eyes walked over to study it. It was masterful and he was sure it had never been on public display.

In the corner was a chaise on which lay a woven lap blanket which was designed with inlaid green and gold threads. An antique Victorian lamp on the table had provided light for her to read or rest by.

He felt that Marisol's spirit still kept the room vibrant and filled with love. He reached out and fingered the gold fringe on the lampshade. Near the lamp, he noticed a small varnished cedar box, a music box, he thought. What music did she like? He opened the rectangular lid and the fragrance of cedar enveloped him. He took the box in both hands and sat on the chaise intending to listen to an old Indian song, "Red is the Rainbow." He imagined Marisol dancing to the tune in the privacy of her weaving room and smiled. It was then that he noticed two letters, tied with a delicate red thread, taped to the bottom of the box.

He glanced around the room, then untied the letters, holding them for a long time as if they were made of antique lace. As gently as he could, he pried one from its envelope. The paper had yellowed with age and the large handwriting had faded somewhat but he could still read the handwriting.

> Marisol, I need you desperately ... I want you with
> all my heart and soul! I love you and yet, as a bright
> star high in the heavens, you are beyond my reach!
> Damn them! Damn all!
>
> Bold Feather

A stunned Eagle Eyes quickly calculated that he had not been born when his father, Bold Feather, had written this to Marisol. He hung his head, sensing the depth and sadness that the solemn declaration of love meant to these two people whose destiny drove them apart, never letting them be united. How he wished he'd gotten the chance to talk to Marisol about his father. How long had she treasured this letter? How many nights had she tiptoed into this adjoining room to read and re-read these poignant lines of unrequited love that his father had written. Love-filled lines that gave her the necessary strength to go on with each day, each hour, each breath. He remembered her words, her calmness, and her delicacy as they waited at the hospital.

So, the tribal rumors of their love were true. He sat a long time, sensing their desperation and their unfulfilled needs. Such loneliness! A tragedy that had run its course for decades, a pain that had never been healed, a sadness that existed for ages.

How different their lives would have been if his father had been able to marry this woman. He wished now that he had coaxed Marisol to speak of her feelings of those times. It might have shed a sympathetic light upon his father's troubled life.

He sighed heavily as he finally opened the next letter. It was just as simple in words but expressed a different love:

Marisol, my shinning star! Your heart and love is
with Bold Feather, but let me try to right what is
wrong. Let me bring a little happiness into your
life. All life must go forward!

Frank Cruz

Eagle Eyes stood and carefully tucked the letters into their envelopes,
then remembered the music box. Which man, he wondered, had given her
the music box? Reverently, he replaced the letters, then closed the small
door and tiptoed out.

He sat on the staircase, feeling the overwhelming burden those letters
pressed upon him. How would Morgana react to the knowledge that the
great love of her mother's life had been Bold Feather? Would she refuse to
acknowledge that Frank Cruz was second in her mother's heart? Did she in
fact know of the letters? As for himself, he sensed the great loss of time and
effort that had gone into a relationship that had never been consummated.

Suddenly, he felt anger. After all, wasn't he Bold Feather's son? Eagle
Eyes felt that his father had had no choice in the matter, since his marriage
had been arranged and he had stood to profit through the transfer of many
acres of high sierra land to his own name.

Frank Cruz could not be faulted, either, for hadn't he provided well
for Marisol as he had promised years back: a fruitful ranch, a gorgeous,
talented daughter. Most important, hadn't Cruz provided a simple, secure
love for Marisol? He leaned his head back to rest against the heavily polished
banister, seeking to find a lesson in this complicated love triangle.

The silence in the house was deafening! His heart pounded loudly, and
his head was dizzy. Still, he needed to decide just how much Morgana meant
to him.

He knew that the night before had been special. He had felt at ease
with her, perhaps, because he was in his own house, free from distracting
conditions. Yes, she had belonged there, in his house, with him. Would she
give all this up to live a simpler life with him at Palo Verde? His hand briskly
brushed his forehead, hoping to massage the problems from his thoughts and
to relieve his tension.

Morgana stood watching him from the top of the staircase. He seemed
so alone sitting in the middle of the stairs with his shoulders hunched-over,
making his head seem heavier than it should be. He was troubled. Gone
was the sun-dancing smile he had possessed so handsomely this morning.
A tightness seemed to penetrate his body. She knew that if she approached
him without forewarning, he would spring like a cougar ready to kill. What
had happened to change his disposition?

"Eagle Eyes," she said softly as she walked slowly down the staircase. "I know you are tired. Why don't you rest?"

He immediately stood and looked up at her as she descended the stairs. She had changed into an old pair of jeans and sweatshirt. Her bare feet made no sound upon the polished stairs as she descended. Dressed so simply, she looked out of place in the elaborate foyer. He stood and leaned against the banister, tightly gripping it for support. "There is something I want to know," he whispered.

She stood slightly above him.

"Do you know about the letters?" he asked.

She looked confused and shrugged. "What letters?"

"Never mind," he answered, then he looked at Morgana. "Do you love me?" he asked in a soft voice.

She laughed nervously, then stopped abruptly realizing that he was serious. "We started off so wrong. Things just happened at the wrong time ... I mean ... I need time." She saw his face pale as his jaw became rigid. "Eagle Eyes, what is going on?"

"If you need time, then see what time can do to a relationship!" Angrily, he grabbed her hand and pulled her into the weaving room. There he turned over the music box to expose the letters, then he handed them to her. "How do you measure time, Morgana?" he yelled bitterly. "Will your love last for eternity as theirs did? Yet, they died apart, alone, still yearning for what could have been something beautiful." He pivoted and stood at the door, watching her stare in confusion at the letters.

"Eagle Eyes, what is wrong?" she said much too late, for he had stormed out of the room. She flinched when she heard the downstairs door slam shut. Her first reaction was to follow him, but the letters caught her attention and she sat down to look at them.

The letters had Marisol's name on each envelope, but she immediately noticed the difference in handwriting. She smiled as she recognized the small elementary scribble. The large handwriting she failed to recognize, so she opened it first.

When she had finished reading Bold Feather's letter, she lay back, dizzy with contemplation. Marisol's love for Bold Feather was something she had briefly mentioned. All Morgana knew was that at one time her mother and Bold Feather had loved each other. She shook her head, not understanding, as she slowly opened her father's letter.

She read his letter proudly. Her father had obviously won this contest of love, for hadn't he married Marisol, hadn't he fulfilled his promise? Yes, Morgana felt that her father was the better man. Her mother had come to her senses and chosen well. More power to him, she mused happily. After a moment, she rigidly sat up, wondering what had prevented Bold Feather from succeeding and winning the hand of Marisol. Calmly, she retreated into her deep memories, but she could not remember hearing a thing about her mother and Bold Feather, not from her father, not from Isadora, nor from Cousin Tom.

This is strange, she thought, for Bold Feather was an important tribal chief once, even if that had been a long time ago. She stood up. Obviously, Eagle Eyes knew something about the affair. She ran to put on her boots, then she went outside to find Eagle Eyes. She'd probe this out of him if it was the last thing she did on earth!

Chapter 14

Morgana rushed out of the house, stopping only to button her leather jacket. Glancing through heavy snow flakes toward the barn, she noticed that Eagle Eyes's truck was no longer parked there. She ran down the slippery path hoping he had moved his truck inside the barn. Then, as she flung open the door to the barn, Cousin Tom rose to greet her.

"Little Cousin, Eagle Eyes has asked me to escort you to the hospital, so anytime you're ready, we'll leave." He walked toward her, noticing her flushed face, wondering what had happened to make Eagle Eyes so hell-fire mad.

"He left, didn't he?" she asked angrily.

Tom merely nodded.

"What a snake he is!" she cried.

A smile crossed Tom's face. "No, cousin, he is no snake. He is an eagle, brutal and fierce, and you are like a new-born lamb to him."

"A lamb! A lamb he would willingly lead to slaughter just as he did Isadora's beautiful mare!" She kicked at a mound of straw on the floor.

Tom laughed. "He is a man. Treat him like a man whom you love instead of like a father which he is not." He put his arm over her shoulder. "I know him. Believe me, he is all that I say he is, and if you wish to win his love, you must give him a love that no other woman can."

"Love! How do you love someone like him? He's bull-headed and always wants his own way!"

"You are the one with your nose tilted toward the sky. You are the privileged one. You have only to request and your wish is granted. He is all that you are not."

"Win his love? I'm sure there are other women in his life," she responded angrily, even though the thought of another woman was something she had not considered. She'd thought of Eagle Eyes as a sacred monk saved by an aging Winter Star.

"Yes, there are several who would lead you to the slaughter to win his admiration, but one in particular, one with whom he has been for a long time before he ever laid eyes upon your fair lips. She is one who pleases him much."

"Good, let her have him!"

111

Tom laughed. "Any man would love to have the sweet . . . Oh, well," he hesitated. "I will not mention her name." His laughter increased when he saw her hazel eyes blaze in anger. "Come, let's go to the hospital." He took her arm. "I understand your father is better." He walked her to the jeep, then went to open the barn door while Morgana sat in the jeep wondering about this woman.

Tom started the engine and slowly moved the jeep into the falling snow. "Do you love him?" he asked soberly, daring not to look directly at her.

Morgana quickly turned to face him. "I thought this other woman loved him!" she snapped quickly, turning her face away from him.

"She does. The question is does he love her or you?" he added. "It's simple, really." He cast her a serious glance. "Do you love him?"

"I guess I'm simple then!" she replied angrily tossing her hair back.

Tom started to laugh.

"Cousin Tom! This is not funny!" she snapped.

"You're right, it's not funny!"

He shifted gears and drove out to the main highway, laughing intermittently, hoping he had not offended his young cousin who only stared out the window refusing to say another word.

Morgana's anger raged during the entire trip to the hospital, yet she dared not explode. Cousin Tom would not know anything about love. After all, he had never married. He spent most of his days painting western scenes of Indians and horses. Well, that was his choice of a lifestyle. Still, her lack of knowledge concerning her relatives on her mother's side of the family disturbed her, making her realize how out of touch with her Indian culture she had really been. She'd make it a point to correct that in the future.

"Are you going to wait for me?" she asked as they left the jeep in the parking lot.

"Yes. We'll go back whenever you're ready." He took her by the elbow and walked alongside. A shy grin still masked his unshaven oval face. "Don't worry, Little Cousin. Your mother is gone, but you have me, and blood is thicker than love!" he chuckled merrily.

Morgana smiled, "Yes, Cousin Tom. Blood is much thicker than love. In a lot of ways you're like Mother. I can remember you standing in the shadows, one eye forever watching her. Why was it like that between you two?" Morgana eased through the doors he had opened for her.

Tom chuckled, "Your mother was kind and gentle like a mist upon a flower. She was older than I, and was such a beautiful girl. I guess I fell in love with her each time she came to visit. I was barely five and she'd hug me, pay attention to me when no one else would. She bought me my first paint set. Now I make more money than I can use from painting."

The elevator doors opened and Morgana moved out ahead of Tom. "Mother wasn't much when it came to talking about other people and their lives. I guess she thought that was akin to being a gossip."

"That sounds like her," Tom added softly.

Morgana approached the nurses' station. "Frank Cruz has gotten out of ICU. What room is he in now?" she asked hurriedly.

A nurse looked through a file case and said, "Room 302, straight down the hallway."

Tom tipped his hat to her, smiled and said, "Thank you." As they walked down the hall he said, "Why don't you go in first, Little Cousin. I'll wait here."

"Sure, Tom." She took a deep breath, then gently pushed open the door. "Father?" she said softly as the door closed behind her.

Frank Cruz lay sleeping. The breathing tubes and oxygen masks were off, but the IV's were still connected to both of his arms. Most of his face was covered with slightly stained bandages, as was his chest. Yet Morgana sensed his breathing was not as labored.

"Father, you're better! You're going to get well! I know it!" She encouragingly searched his closed eyes for any sign of alertness, then reached up and touched his forehead. "Father, you've got to get better. You have to help me with the ranch, remember?" Her voice choked back the tears, and for a long while she merely sat holding his hand, praying over him until Tom entered.

"As you see, he's much better," Morgana said to Tom.

"Yes," Tom agreed. "Time heals all, Morgana." He put his arm on her shoulder. "It's true, Little Cousin. I saw so much in Vietnam and now it seems like it didn't really happen." Tom came closer to the bed. "The doctor is in his office in case you want to talk to him."

"Yes, I need to speak to him." Morgana rose and hurried out the door.

The prognosis the doctor gave Morgana was a bit encouraging and as she walked slowly back to her father's room, she sighed with some relief. Then she glanced at the round-faced clock on the wall outside her father's door. It was already past four in the afternoon, and the still visible white hospital walls would soon turn grey as darkness approached. The halls echoed with the hurried footsteps of the busy staff as they completed their routines. How on earth would he ever recover here, she wondered? In the ICU ward she could hear her blood rushing through her veins. Out on the regular ward, the real world crashed and clanged its way through the nine-to-five routines of the staff.

Morgana decided that at the end of the week, she would take her father home whether or not the doctor advised it. She would even hire a nurse to attend to him for a week or two. He's all I have now, she thought. No one seems to understand that or care about that. He's not an Indian, nor an Anglo. He's my father, a man who really loves me the way I am, and I love him the way he is. She smiled down at her father. "I'm going to take you home, Father, and I'll nurse you back to health."

The door opened and Cousin Tom peeked inside. He stood silent a moment, then said, "Little Cousin, we must leave soon."

Morgana tenderly adjusted the blanket around her father, then kissed him good-bye for the night.

When she got home from the hospital that night, the fire in the fireplace had died down, and a chill settled in the house as she made her way through it. She flicked on the light in every room, thinking she would leave them on until morning. The house loomed larger than ever and she suddenly had an inkling of fear. She knew it was the fear of being totally alone even though Cousin Tom had checked all the doors, making sure they were securely locked before bidding her goodnight. He insisted on sleeping in the barn tonight.

Morgana sat in the brightly lit den and stared at the tapestry her mother had woven. The eyes of the Indian princess seemed so solemn and the chief looked so downcast. The river that divided them appeared to be fierce. Morgana suddenly laughed. So, Mother, she thought, this chief was Bold Feather and this princess was yourself. The lovebirds that were split for eternity. Did Father ever figure this out, she wondered, or was he too busy to stop to analyze the situation?

The doorbell rang. She rose slowly, wondering what Cousin Tom had forgotten. She then went to the foyer and peered out the small window, hurriedly opening the door. "Kelly! What are you doing here?"

Kelly entered the foyer, removing his hat. "Hello! Hope I'm not intruding?"

"I was just sitting in the den. Please come in?" She took his coat and hat and hung them in a small closet. "Are you well enough to be out?"

"Yes, I'm better, thanks." He walked into the den and stood until Morgana 'joined him.

"Would you like a drink?" she asked. "Hot tea or, perhaps, red wine?"

"Wine would be great!" He watched her pour the drink and noticed she'd lost a lot of weight. "How are you, Morgana?"

"I'm fine. Worried about my father, that's all. I've just returned from the hospital. He seems better."

He sat down across from her. "Yes, I just left the hospital. Cruz does seem better. I have to admit that for a while there I was really worried. I'd be dead if ... well, forget it."

They sat in silence for a few moments. Then Kelly rose to relit the fire. "Cruz is a fine man. The loss of Marisol will set him back. I know it'll take a long time for him ... a long, long time." He looked at her. "I'm sorry. I was so concerned about his loss, I ... forgot what you must be going through."

She struggled to control herself as Kelly continued. "I'll be around, if that's any consolation. I owe you for my life. I know this is not the right time, but I would like for you to accept the necklace I wanted you to have in celebration of your good health." He reached into his pocket and pulled out the black velvet box and held it toward her. "As the daughter of my good buddy, and as a token to our long friendship, I plead for you to accept it." She did not reach out to take it, but she did look up into his face. He continued, "Please ... it'll never belong to anyone else ... only to you."

She reached out and took the box, and with her head bowed, she replied, "As the daughter of your good buddy, I accept your gift as a token to my good health. Thank you, Kelly."

He sat down once again and they both remained silent until he said, "He'll not die, Morgana. I can feel that in my bones." He looked around the house. "You know, this place is so large. You'll need a housekeeper, a companion to be with you. Why don't I have my people look for someone suitable. Would you like that?"

She rose. "No. I mean, I plan to bring my father home and I want to hire a nurse to stay with him for a while. The hospital is so noisy and he'll get more rest here."

"Great idea. Let me locate a nurse and you can pay her. I'd want to have her credentials checked first. Is that okay?"

She nodded. "That would be nice, Kelly. I really didn't know where to begin to look. Cousin Tom is taking care of the stock for me, so I don't have to worry about that either."

"Well, looks like things are in order and if you need me, I'm just over the mountain. Pick up the phone and call me."

He rose. "It's late. I must go."

Morgana walked him to the door. "Thanks, Kelly."

He put on his coat and Stetson, "Then we'll probably see each other at the hospital." He hesitated a moment. "Eat something, Morgana. Keep your strength up. You'll need it when he gets home."

She laughed softly. "You're right, Kelly. My father will be raising all sorts of hell when he gets back!"

He kissed her on the forehead. "Good to hear you laugh."

"Thanks for making me laugh." She closed the door and after Kelly was gone, she went back into the den and poured herself a glass of wine. Then she sat staring into the fire.

Later, Morgana went to her bedroom, flicked on the lights and fell on the bed, quietly sobbing. She felt lost and disoriented. Occasionally she'd hear echoes vibrate throughout the house, but in her present state of misery, she ignored them. She wanted her mother to sit here on the bed with her, to soothe her, and to tell her that things would be fine.

"Mother," she whispered, "thank you for being so close to Cousin Tom. I don't know how I would have survived if he had not helped out." Tears ran down her face, but she did not wipe them away. Instead, she pressed her face into her pillow and cried until she exhausted herself. Why shouldn't she feel sorry for herself? After all, she knew she still had to come to terms with her mother's death. "Isadora! Help me heal this pain in my heart!" She rose, went to the bathroom and took a couple of sleeping pills. Finally, she fell into a hard sleep.

As she slept, Morgana saw Isadora coming to her, holding her arms as if to embrace her. Isadora's gown seemed to float weightlessly in the air.

"My child," Isadora whispered. "Cease this crying!"

Beads of perspiration covered Morgana's face. She wanted to fly into Isadora's soothing embrace and to look into Marisol's warm smile once more.

"No!" Isadora commanded. "You should think only of your future. Your father has his own destiny to follow and his own dues to pay. Be brave, Morgana. Be a warrior. You are the seed of fine blood."

Morgana felt she wanted to die, for she wanted to be with Isadora and Marisol. "I cannot go on living!" she screamed to Isadora. "Do you hear me, Isadora?" But Isadora had evaporated into a mist as thick as fog, refusing to listen to her friend's plea.

♡   ♡   ♡

Eagle Eyes had seen Kelly drive out. He noticed that the house was all lit up as if it were ready for a fiesta. What did Kelly want? It was late and he knew he had no business with Morgana that couldn't wait until morning. He stood in the snow suddenly feeling jealous. He wanted to see her, but reluctantly decided against it. Instead, he knocked on the barn, signaling to Tom that he was there.

Tom opened the door enough for him to slide through. "I see you decided to come back. I figured you'd be consoling yourself with your old love."

Eagle Eyes stared at him angrily. "This is no time for jokes, Tom. Your little cousin upsets me so that I cannot be with another woman."

Eagle Eyes sat sullen and silent for a long while, not noticing that Tom was reading his thoughts as if he were following coyote tracks. So, Eagle

Eyes does have a heart for her, Tom concluded, and it seems to me that Morgana loves him too, even though they have fought.

Tom turned to Eagle Eyes. "She is alone now. Why not talk to her? She seems upset, for she did not speak all the way back to the ranch, nor did she sleep." He waited a respectable moment hoping Eagle Eyes would get up and go inside, but his friend did not. He merely sat there, staring into the lantern light.

"Is she not worth fighting for?" Tom questioned seriously.

"She is beautiful and she disturbs me more than any other woman, but she is half-clan."

Tom laughed. "Oh, I see. Well then, the matter is settled. She is not good enough for an Indian of such an established character as yourself, but she is good enough for that white man to win, just as her mother was good enough for the Mexican." Angrily, Tom lashed out. "I thought you were a better man! Have you not learned a lesson from Marisol and Bold Feather? Real love is much better than a marriage with someone you do not love. Can't you see that? Is land and a position in tribal matters more important than to have someone love you regardless of who or what you are? Eagle Eyes, you are not thinking!"

If knives had been thrown, the stare that Eagle Eyes cast would have killed Tom in an instant. He rose and walked angrily past Tom and slipped out of the barn.

After a few seconds, Tom heard the truck start up, then move slowly up the drive. So, he thought, Eagle Eyes has left. Perhaps he is not such a warrior where women are concerned. Tom was extremely disappointed in his friend. He glanced at this watch. It was well after two in the early morning.

He decided to check the house and to see if all was well with Morgana. As he walked cautiously to the house, the moonlight occasionally peeked through the steady falling mist of snowflakes. He shivered, pulling his coat tighter as he peered at each boulder, shrub and tree while he moved at a slow, safe pace.

Tom hesitated as he reached the doors leading inside the house and glanced around making sure all was quiet. Then he entered the foyer and stood smiling to himself. Morgana must be frightened, for she'd left every light on inside the house. How silly! Didn't she realize he'd be there for her? Even so, he checked each and every room ... just to be on the safe side.

Tom repeatedly knocked on Morgana's bedroom door but he did not get a response. "Morgana!" he called. After waiting a long interval, he opened the door and entered the room, which was filled with light, only to find that the window was opened wide. He immediately felt the cold and shivered at the sight of Morgana curled on her bed in a fetal position. The comforter was flung on the floor and she tightly hugged her pillow. Her eyes were closed and her face glowed with beads of perspiration as if the heavens had dusted her face with silvery stars. Tom touched her forehead and noticed that her skin was hot to the touch in spite of the coldness in the room. He pulled up the comforter and covered her. Then he rushed to close the window. Worried about her, he sat solemnly on the edge of the bed thinking. She had been fine when he'd left her, but that was hours ago. Then, she had seemed a little sad, but that was to be expected, considering her father's condition. Tom called to her, "Morgana, wake up. Do you hear me? Wake up Morgana!" When he failed to rouse her, he wondered what he should do. Could it be, he thought, that the spirit of the dead is haunting her, making her physically and spiritually ill?

Isadora and Marisol had been important women in Morgana's life and as much as he loved his cousin Marisol, Tom knew she was capable of coming back to disturb her daughter out of her desperate love to be near her. Isadora, he knew, also had the power to do just that and, he felt, she too would encourage Morgana to explore the spirit world to communicate with them. Tom knew that it did not take long for the spirit sickness to penetrate the body.

He rose and slammed his fist against the bed post. He should burn this house down to dispose of Isadora and Marisol's spirits quickly, before any more damage could be done to Morgana! Isadora told him years ago when he went away to the war never to take anything off the body of a dead person. "Do this, Tom," she had said, "to show respect for the dead and they, in turn, shall not haunt or harm you. It is but a simple way of letting them know that they have received your respect."

He glanced down at Morgana who had not moved since he'd entered the room. Carefully, he felt her pulse, noting its weakness. She needed a cleansing, a sweat bath, he thought. He quickly glanced around the room, found the phone and dialed Eagle Eye's home. After several rings, Winter Star answered.

"No!" she replied. He was not home, but she herself was once schooled in the traditional sweat ceremony and would gladly help if Tom could bring Morgana to her.

"Wrap her warmly!" she advised. "Smear black soot from ashes over her cheeks."

"I'll do that, Winter Star. Then," he added, "I'll burn this place down!"

"Tom!" she warned. "It is not her place, nor is she dead. We must tend to her first," she commanded. "I shall be ready to begin the ceremony as soon as you arrive. In the meantime, I'll call around for Rusty."

♡   ♡   ♡

Tom carried Morgana to the hut where Winter Star lived. The old woman greeted him and directed him to a rear room outside the hut. Winter Star looked strange, he thought, as he carried Morgana in the direction the old woman led him. It was the first time he'd ever seen Winter Star with her long silver hair unbraided and hanging straight down. He placed Morgana on a small mat and glanced at the steaming hot stones. The tiny room was very hot.

"Where is Eagle Eyes?" he asked Winter Star.

"I could not find him," she replied, then added, "Go away, Tom. I have much to do." Winter Star shoved him out the door, then turned to Morgana. She dipped water from a circular pearl shell and carefully poured it over the hot stones, creating a rush of steam that quickly enveloped the room. Winter Star turned to the motionless Morgana, sponging her face and praying as she performed the ceremony that hopefully would improve Morgana's health.

Chapter 15

Tom felt extremely betrayed because Eagle Eyes was not there to help Winter Star at a time when both she and Morgana really needed him. He got into his jeep and sped out to the highway, heading for the secluded spot where he thought Eagle Eyes might be found, a spot they had discovered many years ago. Both men frequented the deserted place to be alone whenever they needed time to think or to sort out their problems. As he maneuvered the jeep carefully over the snow-covered highway, he visualized Eagle Eyes sitting cross-legged, covered by a thick blanket and staring out across the moonlit mesa. Perhaps Eagle Eyes would be humming an Indian war song. Perhaps he would not speak at all. That was his way. But, should he be there, it would be because he wanted to heal his own wounds and to withdraw from the troubled world. A slow smile crept upon Tom's face as he realized that he would no doubt find Eagle Eyes there.

Tom parked the jeep and immediately saw Eagle Eyes' truck. Then he made his way up the slippery path until the terrain leveled off. For a moment he had a difficult time distinguishing Eagle Eyes because of the falling snow and the many branches that protected the small entrance. His friend was snuggled beneath a blanket covered with snow. Eagle Eyes looked back when he heard Tom approach.

"Eagle Eyes, I have found you. May I disturb your prayers?"

"I am not praying. I am thinking."

Tom sat a small distance away from him. After a long while, he said, "She is at your house. I suspect she has the sickness—the spirit sickness!"

Eagle Eyes wiped his eyes, then stared at Tom waiting for an explanation.

"When I phoned I asked for you, but Winter Star insisted that she could do the sweat ceremony."

Eagle Eyes rose, flung off the blanket and turned toward the path. Suddenly he stopped and asked, "Aren't you coming?"

Tom sat silent a moment. "Go, you can make it down the path faster than I. Morgana needs you." Judging from Eagle Eyes's anxiety to hurry down the path, Tom wondered if Winter Star was knowledgeable enough to perform the Healing Ghost-Way Ceremonial. He hoped so, for if it were performed inaccurately there would be dangers to confront. But, he trusted Eagle Eyes as a healer and knew he could handle any situation that might emerge. He rose and took a moment to glance at the snow-covered mountains. Mother Earth was waking and it promised to be a crisp, cold day. Cousin Tom gave thanks by raising his hands in prayer to the heavens.

♡   ♡   ♡

Eagle Eyes shoved open the door to the hut with such force that the door cracked. A gust of steam greeted him as if it were a bellowing storm cloud. The steam was so thick that he could not see Winter Star or Morgana. He walked blindly a few steps forward feeling what he could with the tip of his boot. "Winter Star!" he cried. "You have put too much water upon the hot stones. Winter Star, do you hear me!"

"Rusty ... " Winter Star answered.

He carefully circled the pit of hot stones until he touched her. "It's all right now, Winter Star, I'm here. Everything will be fine."

"What is wrong?" Morgana asked as she peered up at Eagle Eyes through the thinning mist.

"Morgana?" Eagle Eyes said. "How do you feel? Tom told me you were ill."

"I took some sleeping pills. I guess I took one too many."

Eagle Eyes looked over at her seriously. "You scared the pants off Tom. He thought you needed a ... special sweat." He sat directly across from her and smiled through the thinning mist.

"She's fine," added Winter Star.

"I was enjoying my sweat with Winter Star. She told me that Tom could not wake me. It was the pills. Winter Star sponged water on my face and that woke me," she explained nervously.

"How many pills did you take?" he asked.

"I took two. The pills belonged to Mother. I guess they were pretty strong. I kept thinking about Mother and Isadora. It upset me. Even the house seemed to vibrate with their voices. My nerves were shot and then there was the problem with ... you."

Winter Star rose. "I will leave now." She moved around Eagle Eyes and affectionately patted him on the shoulder. "I sleep now," she said.

After Winter Star left, Eagle Eyes continued, "You mentioned a problem concerning me."

Morgana glanced down at the cooling rocks that formed a circle. She tried desperately to contain the emotions that were bursting inside her. "You rushed off like a fool and did not allow me time for an explanation. I went to the barn looking for you, but you'd hurried off to God knows where. I mean, is it my fault my mother decided to marry my father and could not marry your father? No. I am innocent. And, another thing, I am not your sister or half-sister!"

Eagle Eyes raised both arms in a gesture of peace. "I never believed those rumors that you were my sister. Yes, I had heard them, but I knew they were false. Isadora told me long ago that the talk was false, that your mother was unjustly maligned. I liked your mother very much. I wish I could have known her better, but I did not have that opportunity just as I did not have the opportunity to know my own father."

In a sad voice Morgana continued. "Those letters must have been special to Mother, and I feel I have violated her privacy." She sighed. "Nevertheless, I will keep them forever."

"I am honored that you will keep my father's letter."

Morgana glanced up into Eagle Eye's eyes and noticed the slow smile that had crept upon his face. She blushed and glanced down at her clasped hands.

After a long moment of silence he said, "You are once again a guest in my house." He waited to see if she would raise her eyes to meet his gaze. When she didn't, he continued, "Morgana, I have decided that we must marry."

She quickly gasped, "You have decided this?"

"Yes, I have decided that ... I love you." he added in a firm tone, yet looking at the circle of rocks.

"Eagle Eyes! We must decide this matter together!"

"Yes, you are right. So decide," he added seriously.

She laughed when she saw that Eagle Eyes continuously pulled at his shirt cuff. "Okay, it's my turn to decide." She purposely hesitated a long while, staring at the steaming stones before her. "I have decided," she added as she looked over at him.

"And, what is your answer?" he questioned, as his serious glance faltered into one of agony.

"I have decided that I love you, too."

He merely nodded as the relief flooded throughout his body and he relaxed. "It is good."

"Yes," she added, "And, I have decided one more thing."

He glanced at her anxiously, "What?"

"I have decided that we must marry tonight."

He laughed. "Unbelievable! You want to marry tonight?"

"Why not?" she reasoned, "Since father is ill, he cannot attend. Isn't a wedding a gathering of the most important people in one's life? I believe so. Isadora is dead and Mother is also gone. Winter Star is here and Cousin Tom is on his way. Other people are not as important."

He stared at her a long while. "Are you serious?"

She nodded. "Yes, Eagle Eyes. I am serious."

"Then, it shall be tonight! I will make the arrangements. We shall marry here. I will call the old Chief." He hesitated, then asked, "Are you well enough to go through a Navajo ceremony?"

"I can manage it. I will miss my father, but we can re-marry in the Mexican tradition later. Would you do this for me?" she asked.

He smiled, then hesitated a long moment. "I am not Mexican, but if it makes peace for the three of us, then I shall be honored."

She studied his face. "You are not angry that I asked this?"

He smiled. "No."

She reached over the cooling rocks and gently touched his dimpled chin, then passed her finger over his lips.

He kissed the palm of her hand. "If we are to marry tonight, we must get started on the preparations," he added gently.

"You are right," she replied, withdrawing her hand.

He stood and quickly stepped over the rocks. He gently pulled her to her feet, then took her face in his hands and kissed her. "I shall not give up my medicine, nor my position with the tribal legal service. I say this now because both require my time at different hours of the day. Sometimes at night as well. You must never be jealous of my two work masters, for when they call I must go." He grasped her snugly around the waist and pulled her closer to him.

"So be it." She put her arms around his neck. "And, I shall be your third master."

"So be it."

♡   ♡   ♡

Winter Star was crazy with delight when Eagle Eyes told her that he and Morgana would be wed at sunset. She clapped her hands and danced around the kitchen until she could no longer stand, then she landed breathlessly into a chair. "Ho!" she gasped. "I have much food to prepare. I shall start now."

Eagle Eyes laughed at her while he dialed the old Chief's telephone number. "There shall not be many guests, Winter Star."

"That will not prevent me from making a splendid Indian dinner," she exclaimed, continuing to clap her hands together playfully.

"As you like, Winter Star," he added. "If you need anything, tell Tom. He shall be leaving to pick up a very special dress for Morgana."

"Ah, where is this dress coming from?" Winter Star asked curiously.

"It's a gift," he replied.

"From Isadora, no?"

He nodded, then turned his attention to the Chief's voice over the receiver. A smile beamed brightly on his face when the Chief agreed to do the ceremony on such short notice. He had expected an inquisition as to why the wedding needed to be performed with such haste, but when Eagle Eyes explained that it was Morgana Cruz, Marisol's daughter, the Chief agreed.

"Yes," commented the old Chief. "I knew her mother well. If you are sure that Morgana is the woman you wish to marry, then I would be glad to be at the house before sunset to perform the ceremony. I will also bring the drummer. Would Eagle Eyes welcome the Chief's wife as well?"

"Yes! Please bring her and anyone else you wish. It will be my honor to serve you and your clan." Eagle Eyes was pleased that the Chief felt comfortable enough to bring his favored ones.

Winter Star could tell that Eagle Eyes was pleased, as his facial features took on a humble glow. When he hung up the phone, she asked, "Now, Rusty ... tell me of her dress."

"Do not worry, Winter Star. It is as if Isadora foresaw this marriage." He picked her up and whirled her around. "Isadora made a dress. She gave it to me shortly before she passed and said that she would be eternally happy if my future wife were to wear the dress."

The old woman sniffled. "Ah, I believe Isadora has reached down from her spirit world to make sure all things go well for you both. It is good."

♡   ♡   ♡

Morgana shampooed her hair and showered slowly. Then, after both tasks were completed, she felt dizzy and light-headed and instinctively supported herself by leaning against the shower tiles, letting the water massage her tense muscles. Afterwards, she dressed but felt too exhausted to do much more than sit on the bed and nibble at the food that Winter Star had placed on the dresser. She thought only of lying down when a knock at the door startled her.

"Morgana," Tom called. "May I come in?"

"Yes, Tom," she answered.

Tom stood at the door smiling. "I am pleased for you and for my best friend." He went to her and hugged her tightly. "Tonight, I shall attend the wedding of the two people that I love most in this world; but first I must go to Santa Fe. Is there anything I can get for you?"

"Would you mind stopping at the ranch?"

"I'm going there first to tend to the animals. What do you need?"

"Recently I completed a vase. It is in my workshop, on top of my workbench. My keys are on top of the dresser in my room. Open the shop and get the vase. It will be my gift to Eagle Eyes."

He smiled. "Wasn't this vase to go to Bo, your dealer, to be sold for a good price?"

"Yes, but now it is a gift from my heart to my husband-to-be."

Chapter 16

The pink and blue rays of the approaching sunset marked the sky as Morgana finished dressing for the ceremony. She stood straight while Winter Star skirted around her, fussing, pulling here and tucking there. Morgana smiled as Winter Star assisted her with the satin turquoise blouse which was decorated with gold coins all lined in a row down each sleeve. The blouse did not have the traditional collar of most Navajo blouses, for Isadora had scalloped it into a low "V" down the front which she had edged with delicate gold thread. Winter Star then pulled over Morgana's head a black velvet ankle length skirt gathered slightly at the waist.

"It fits perfectly!" Morgana turned to get a full view of herself. "It is as if Isadora had measured every inch of me."

"So it is," added Winter Star. She giggled happily before adding, "Now, for a wedding present for you from my Rusty. The present is very special. It belonged to his father and to his grandfather." She held out an oblong wooden box that gleamed from constant polishing. Morgana glanced down into the twinkling eyes of Winter Star.

"Open it, my child. It is almost time for us to move to the large room for the ceremony."

Morgana slowly opened the lid of the box and gasped, "It's beautiful!"

"Yes, yes!" Winter Star put the box down and lifted out the thick leather belt studded with large silver conchos, each intricately designed with a different bird.

Morgana reached down and ran her finger over the delicate image of a hummingbird perched on a branch. The design of the next five-inch circular silver concho caught her eyes, for it was that of a perched eagle. Surprised, she studied it closer and kept running her finger over it. Somehow, it felt familiar. She studied the other birds: a red bird with a garnet eye, a blue bird embossed in turquoise.

"Hurry, child!" Winter Star insisted, but Morgana stood silent, letting her mind float to where she'd seen the eagle before. It came to her slowly as she recalled that the chief on her mother's tapestry wore the same emblem on his necklace.

"Let's put it on!" Winter Star declared as she slipped the belt around Morgana's waist.

Morgana stared at the reflection of the belt in the mirror, thinking of how her mother must have loved Bold Feather for such a long time. How many years had Bold Feather lived like an invisible spirit within our house, she wondered. The sadness she felt was for herself and for her father. She wondered how much her father knew and how much he had merely ignored in order to keep peace with her mother. Yet Marisol had been faithful to her husband and had stayed with them as their caregiver, always honoring Frank Cruz.

"My child, is something wrong?" Winter Star asked.

"Wrong? No ... ," she softly responded. "But, the belt is heavy."

Winter Star then reached up and slipped a turquoise and silver beaded headband over Morgana's head. She fanned out her long hair, then admiringly patted her shoulder. "You are so ... beautiful!"

Morgana immediately hugged the old woman. "Oh, Winter Star, you are so good." She kissed her forehead. "Now, you will be my mother. You have encircled me with your warmth, your love and care."

Winter Star wailed, "I am a happy old woman."

Just then they heard Tom's voice calling out, "It is time!"

Winter Star opened the door and Tom looked surprised as he admired Morgana. Then he whispered, "Like your mother, you are truly an Indian Princess."

"Cousin Tom, I am glad that you are here to give me away." Morgana took his arm and entered the hall.

"I have called the hospital. Your father is better. They will call if there is any change." He felt Morgana tense up and quickly added, "But never mind ... this is your time."

Her hand tightly gripped his arm. "Yes," she softly replied. "It is my time." She tiptoed to kiss Tom's cheek.

The high-pitched sound of an Indian flute signaled that everyone was in place for the ceremony. The drums rolled, signifying that the husband-to-be had entered the house from the north door. Tom quickly added, "I will always be available if you or Eagle Eyes should need me."

She nodded, unable to speak. Tom gently patted her hand.

The lights dimmed and for a moment there was nothing but silence. At last, a beautiful tune as delicate as the hum of a hummingbird echoed throughout the house. One flute serenaded the wife to be, a second and a third flute joined the joyous melody. The calling of the three Indian flutes was delicate, sweet, promising. Old Navajo lore stated that the girl would fall in love with the boy as he serenaded her with a flute made from the stalk of a sunflower. The harmonious cadence flew upward and outward, directed toward the heavens and earth, sending blessings, praise, energy, light and love.

The drums softly joined in the harmony, adding a masculine tone to the wedding song as they became a part of all that is delicate, all this is soft, all that the loving couple promised to bring to their sacred union.

The Chief glanced affectionately at his wife of many years and she sent back an encouraging wink.

Winter Star, who had followed Rusty as he entered the house from the north, gazed lovingly at him, her Eagle Eyes, the son given to her by Isadora. Her eyes filled with tears which she repeatedly dabbed.

Eagle Eyes nervously pulled at the left sleeve of his silk shirt. His vest, an intricate gold pattern woven upon blue silk, was filled with the sacred colors of the Navajo—the red, the turquoise, the yellow, the black and the white. He, too, glanced nervously at the Chief who stood before him, then he took a deep breath and closed his eyes for a moment, his anticipation, his anxiety reaching a high he'd never experienced.

Eagle Eyes could not believe he stood there waiting to wed such a beautiful, accomplished young woman, a woman who was a well-known master craftsman in pottery, a woman who spoke Navajo, Spanish and English and could interact with any crowd. He thought of Isadora and of her profound wisdom in all matters. How he missed her! How he would have loved to have had her standing next to the Chief witnessing this ceremony.

As he glanced toward the door waiting for the Indian flutes to cease and for Morgana to appear, he felt Isadora's nearness and her love. Inconspicuously he wiped away a stray tear. It would not do for him to cry at this moment, not now, he warned himself, even though his heart felt like bursting. He knew that from now on he would never be alone. She would be there. She would be his family. She would create his home.

Morgana walked down the hallway and entered the large room from the southside, as was decreed. She stood radiant in the middle of more candles than she could count. Cousin Tom lent her support as they stood waiting under the archway leading to the large room. As she waited for the flutes to stop, she quickly surveyed the small intimate group of people and was pleased. For her, this was a very personal affair. She was glad that for now, at least, it would not be the grandiose "wedding fiesta" consisting of dozens of *padrinos*, hundreds of invited guests, a massive cake and a formal dinner and dance that her father would insist upon as his contribution to her wedding celebration. The thought of such an affair made her suddenly very tired. But, nevertheless, she missed her doting father.

She glanced over to where Eagle Eyes stood. He had just turned back, his eyes eager to find her, his eyebrows lifted slightly and his lips slowly curved upward in a smile. Their gazes locked and from that moment on, his eyes never left her. Cousin Tom stopped and lifted a flat basket which contained a small amount of corn mush, which he handed to Morgana. He smiled encouragingly at her, then urged her to move forward to join Eagle Eyes. In front of Eagle Eyes's feet, she placed the basket. Then she rose slowly and moved to his right side.

They stood silently facing the impressively dressed tribal Chief who, with his staff, gently tapped the celebrants on their left shoulder to draw their attention before chanting the Blessing Ceremonial Song. The chant was accompanied by one flute and one Indian drum. The Chief's rich voice, trained from singing at so many ceremonies and pow-wows, caused the nearby candlelight to flicker and flutter.

Then the wife of the Chief brought a jug and placed it in front of the couple. The Chief took the gourd ladle and gave it to Morgana. Then he carefully poured water into it. "Now, Morgana, you may wash his hands."

Nervously Morgana poured water over Eagle Eye's cupped hands and then handed him a small towel with which to dry them. She smiled shyly as she held out the gourd ladle to the Chief.

Eagle Eyes waited for the Chief to refill the gourd ladle. Then he took it from the Chief's hands and poured water on Morgana's hands, watching her as she timidly washed them. He handed her a towel to dry them and turned his attention back to the Chief.

From his leather bag, the Chief took out corn pollen. Morgana took the flat, circular woven basket which Winter Star handed her, while the Chief explained that the circular design on the basket depicted the traditional incomplete Navajo circle which allowed evil to escape and good to enter. Morgana gracefully held the basket out to the Chief as if she were serving a king. The Chief took a pinch of pollen and sprinkled it from east to west over the corn mush, then from north to south. Next he made a small clockwise pollen circle around the basket. "Is there anyone here who objects to my turning the basket halfway around?" He paused. "My friends," he added, "by turning the basket I have turned the minds of the bride and groom toward each other. It is the Navajo way."

After turning the basket, the Chief commanded, "Eagle Eyes, please take a pinch of the corn mush at the edge where the pollen ends towards the East." He pointed to the area.

Eagle Eyes slowly pinched the moist corn mush and put some into his mouth as he watched the Chief move the basket in front of Morgana.

"Morgana, please take a pinch of the corn mush at the edge where the pollen ends towards the East." He again pointed to the area and smiled as Morgana obediently put the mush into her mouth.

Together Eagle Eyes and Morgana took a pinch of corn mush from the South, the West and the North and, finally, both partook of the center where the two lines of pollen crossed.

The Chief took the flat basket and dutifully handed it to Winter Star. "Now, mother of Eagle Eyes, this basket belongs to you for life."

The Chief asked his wife to approach them. "It is time for us to instruct this couple as to their required future conduct toward each other and of their marriage duties. Everyone may sit." In hushed tones the four of them sat together on the floor and discussed marital ethics. Eagle Eyes spoke in hushed whispers while Morgana blushed.

After the instruction, it was time for them to profess their love for one another. The Chief placed his staff on Morgana's shoulder. She had not bothered to memorize any lines, hoping that her feelings would carry her through the moment. As she turned to face Eagle Eyes, she looked up to meet his glance and, for a moment, she lost track of time.

At long last she spoke slowly in Navajo. "Eagle Eyes," she declared in such a soft voice that the Chief leaned forward to better hear her. "I accept you as my lover, my protector, my guide, and above all my partner in this life. I accept your children, your family, and the tribal customs." She hesitated a moment as she suddenly felt his palms sweat. "May all we two do as a couple add to the harmony and peace of those around us so that the Great Spirit may send his showers filled with blessings."

The Chief then placed his staff upon Eagle Eyes's shoulder. Eagle Eyes nervously cleared his throat before he said, "Morgana Cruz, I give you all that I possess—my love, my lands, my cattle and my sheep. I expect heirs and a generous wife who behaves in the proper Indian way. I take you as my companion for as long as we are destined for this world." His hands trembled as he gazed into her eyes which suddenly sparkled with tears. "I love you," he whispered so softly that only she could hear.

The Chief removed his staff and handed Morgana a small basket, newly woven, which symbolized the fetching of the family's food. She curtsied low after accepting the basket.

To Eagle Eyes he handed an arrow, a symbol of the great Indian hunters. Eagle Eyes accepted the arrow and the Chief's embrace.

A book the size of a very large Bible was brought forward. It contained the names and dates of all tribal weddings. He handed Eagle Eyes a pen so he could sign his name; then he offered Morgana the pen to let her also sign her name. She hesitated and whispered to the Chief, "But, I am not full blood."

The Chief quietly responded, "It is known and noted by your mother's records. You may sign for the benefit of your children, so that they too will sign one day."

"So be it." Eagle Eyes prodded her to sign.

"Is my father's name in this book?" she dared ask.

The Chief bent forward. "Yes. He signed to please Marisol."

"Then I shall sign," she added as she hastily wrote her name, suddenly realizing that she'd been listed as a member of the tribe all along. For years she had considered herself an outcast, not really belonging to her mother's clan. She realized now that she had branded herself. Now, to find that her name and the name of her father has been recorded in tribal records overwhelmed her. She turned to look at Eagle Eyes and noticed that he was watching her in wonder.

She smiled, then turned to the Chief who was holding the wedding vase she had recently completed. In the light of so many candles, it shimmered with vibrations. She heard mutterings from the guests as the vase was filled with blessed wine and held high for all to see.

Eagle Eyes leaned to her. "Isadora taught you well. It is a beauty."

The Chief spoke in tones that resounded throughout the room. "In this beautiful wedding vase made by these dedicated hands of the lady of the hour, I have placed the sacred wine." He turned to Eagle Eyes and handed him the vase.

Eagle Eyes slowly turned to face Morgana. He raised the left side of the vase to his lips and sipped. He then handed her the vase and she lifted it to her lips. Indeed, she thought, it sends shivers through my body. It is as I had hoped.

The Chief then took the vase and sipped from the side where all the men sipped and handed it to his wife who sipped from the side where all the women sipped. The Chief's wife took it to Tom who tasted the wine, as did Winter Star. From there, the vase was passed from hand to hand to all the other guests who softly voiced their appreciation. During this time Morgana and Eagle Eyes faced each other holding hands, smiling and glancing occasionally at Winter Star and at Tom. When the vase had made full circle, the Chief placed his hand over their heads and chanted, "Now, you are one. It is as it should be."

Eagle Eyes took Morgana in his arms. "I love you," he said softly.

"I love you, my husband," she added as she accepted his gentle kiss, feeling his heart pound so thunderously that she pulled away slightly. "Is everything all right?" she asked apprehensively.

"Yes, all is well," he whispered in her ear as they turned to receive their guests.

After a superb dinner of cow's tongue, corn on the cob, Indian pudding and corn cakes prepared by Winter Star, more wine was served. Finally the

Chief and his wife rose to leave, and Eagle Eyes and Morgana walked them to the door. "It was a fine wedding. You both are blessed," added the Chief. "Take care of one another, for our times are dangerous."

Soon all the guests departed and only Cousin Tom and Winter Star remained to clean up in the kitchen. Eagle Eyes took Morgana's hand and rushed into the kitchen. He took Winter Star in his arms and said, "Leave this kitchen until tomorrow. Go to your hut and rest, my dear mother."

Winter Star, knowledgeable in the ways of young love, smiled, "Ah, yes ... tomorrow is good. Lots of tomorrows, but for now you two must stay the traditional four nights and four days in this house." She glanced at him and then at Morgana.

Eagle Eyes laughed. "Okay, my mother, but only if fate declares no immediate disasters that I must tend."

Winter Star frowned, but Tom quickly said, "I will walk Winter Star across the way and then I shall go home to my place, for I have missed it." He went to Morgana to kiss her. "Good night, my cousin," he said, then turned to Eagle Eyes and shook his hand. "Congratulations, my friend, you still have your neck attached to your head." Then he grabbed Winter Star in his arms. "I shall carry you home, as if you were my bride."

"Silly boy!" scolded Winter Star as she put her arms around his neck while Eagle Eyes covered her with a blanket. "Such silly boys!" she giggled happily.

Eagle Eyes and Morgana stood watching Winter Star and Tom as they made their way down the path to her hut.

"Now, my wife, I shall carry you over the threshold of our bedroom." He easily lifted her into his arms.

"Really, Eagle Eyes," she laughingly asked, "We married in the Indian way and, now, you're enacting a traditional Western custom." She kissed his cheek as he lifted her and walked down the hallway.

"We are of both worlds, I think," he added pensively. "So we can get away with doing things that others cannot."

"And now," she asked, "we need to tell my father that we are married."

"That's the first thing we must do tomorrow," he replied.

♡   ♡   ♡

Cruz opened his eyes. "*¡Dios!*" His chest ached and his jaw throbbed. He was remembering the turmoil on the mountain top and thus, feeling fear for Kelly and Santos.

At that moment the door to his room slowly opened. "Cruz!" Kelly said in relief, "you're awake!"

Cruz took Kelly's hand and gently held it, relieved that his friend was alive and obviously well.

"I thought we'd lost you," Kelly said as he felt a squeeze from the old man's hand. Feeling nostalgic, he added, "Remember the first time we met? At the campsite just before nightfall? We shared hot coffee and fried fish."

Cruz squeezed his hand and managed to whisper, "Yes." He tried to smile, but the pain was too great. "Yes, *compadre*," he said, then humorously asked, "Have you got something to eat?"

Kelly laughed. "Morgana will be pleased that you're so snappy."

"Where is she?" Cruz whispered, letting his eyes move toward the door.

Kelly cleared his throat nervously, "She is on her way here. Listen, I'll check on you tomorrow, *amigo*," he said as he put on his Stetson to leave, then added, "You and I are going deep sea fishing in Cancún. The trip is on me, *compadre*. I hear it's especially nice down there in December about Christmas time. So, hurry and get well. See you tomorrow!"

No sooner had Kelly left than Eagle Eyes and Morgana walked down the hall, hand in hand, toward Frank Cruz's room. At the door, Eagle Eyes hesitated a moment, but Morgana encouraged him to enter. She then approached the bed and kissed her father on the cheek. "Father, I'm so happy you're better!"

Cruz's eyes fixed on her. He reached for her hand, bringing it to his cheek. Then his eyes turned toward Eagle Eyes. "Father," Morgana quickly blurted out, "Eagle Eyes and I got married." She lifted her hand out to Eagle Eyes, who immediately took it.

Cruz's eyes loomed larger than ever as they sized up Eagle Eyes. "So," he whispered, "you have married my daughter?"

"Yes," Eagle Eyes replied, "I love her and I will honor her."

Cruz's eyes filled with tears. "*Hija*, do you love him?"

"I love him and I love you too," Morgana replied softly.

Cruz put his hand to her cheek. "I want you to be happy." He then lifted his hand to Eagle Eyes.

Eagle Eyes grasped it firmly. "Thank you, sir," he replied.

Then Cruz looked towards the door. "Where's your mother?" he asked.

"Father," Morgana hesitated, "I have to tell you … Mother died a few days ago."

Before Cruz could fully react, Eagle Eyes moved quickly, trying to prevent Cruz from sitting up.

Morgana hugged her father. "The doctor said she died from heart failure. It happened so quickly. There was nothing anyone could do. I'm so sorry that you have to find it out this way, especially when you're still recuperating from your horrible accident." Morgana laid her head upon her father's chest and quietly sobbed.

Cruz shut his eyes tightly as tears ran down his cheeks. "Not her," he said softly.

Eagle Eyes stepped away, allowing father and daughter privacy to express their grief together. He stood with his back to them looking out the window, thinking of his own mother, his aunt, Isadora, and Winter Star and of how all these women had given meaning to his life. Silently he honored them.

After a long while, Eagle Eyes felt Morgana gently touch his shoulder. "He's sleeping," she whispered.

"Good," Eagle Eyes said, putting his arms around her.

She smiled at him. "You and I will help Father adjust to his new life. It will be hard for him, but he is a strong man."

"Yes," replied Eagle Eyes. "Together, we can do it."

"That's how it should be," whispered Morgana taking hold of Eagle Eyes's hand. "Now, we three are a family."